The Woman In The Window

All of the stories in *The Woman In The Window* are works of fiction. All of the names, characters and events are the product of the author's imagination. Any resemblance to true events or real people, living or dead, is purely coincidental.

Copyright © 2016 W. D. Fyfe
Excerpt from *No Safe Harbors* © 2016 W.D. Fyfe

All rights reserved. This book or any portion thereof may not be reproduced or used in any manner whatsoever without the express written permission of the author -- except for the use of brief quotations in a book review.

ISBN - 13: 978-1539372387
ISBN - 10: 1539372383

To Kay --
You know what you've done.

....Introduction

Short stories are not an extended journey; they're an afternoon stroll. You can read them in less than a sun tan on a hot afternoon or finish them quite easily over a second cup of coffee on a lazy Sunday morning. They're a lunch hour in the park or a read before sleep. Yet for all their convenience, short stories are clever little things. They're tightly woven tales that are all in one place, all at the same time.

The Woman In The Window is not about relationships. It's about the delicious ache in the bottom of your belly -- that sweet primeval that won't go away; the wolf of our emotions, hungry and hunting. These eight tales are about people who have been living their lives cocooned in their accumulated habits, but suddenly, by chance or by choice, they travel beyond the reach of their familiar world. Without the thin cloak of everyday life around them, they find themselves alone in the wilderness, trying to understand whether they are prey or predator.

In "The Last Romance Of Jasper Conrad," Frances says to Jasper, "Just – just because I'm ordinary doesn't mean I can't have something more. I look around and I see my life and ..." But Frances isn't ordinary, and Jasper knows that.

In "The Dying of Daniel," when Susan asks "... God, are we ever going to be normal?" Peter replies, "Normal? Normal just happens.... There's nothing you can do about it." But for Susan there is no normal, and there never has been.

"Ordinary," "normal," "average:" these are words we use to protect ourselves. They keep our emotions, our imagination and our sensuality at bay. However, as the characters in *The Woman In The Window* discover, in the sleepless soul of 4 o'clock in the morning, these words are meaningless. The truth is, we are all only as ordinary as we require ourselves to be.

Vancouver, 2016

Table of Contents

1....Roman Holiday

25....Scars*

41....The Ballad of Lisa and Lacey

79....The Bookstore on Elliott Street

97....Final Vinyl Cafe

115....The Dying of Daniel

143....The Last Romance of Jasper Conrad

189....A Simple Thing

*The original version of "Scars" was published in Quality Women's Fiction Magazine.

....Roman Holiday

She loved the look of the street at night. Deep dark, patched together with dull blocks of light from the shops and restaurants; the street lamps and traffic lights sliding over everything that moved. Everyone down there slowly settling in after feeding the tourists. The bustle gone and the real sounds and noises of the city finally drifting up to her as the foreigners got safely tucked into their beds. Not that she minded tourists; she didn't. Even after all these years (how many had it been? – twenty) they still reminded her of home. Although home didn't really mean home anymore. Home really didn't mean anything. This was home. That was home. When you spend your whole life on vacation, anywhere is home. In all, she preferred Paris, but Rome was Rome and she owned the apartment and she was four floors up over Via Cavour, and you just can't get a bad bottle of wine in Italy. Besides, it was a beautiful warm summer night, and somewhere down there, mingled in the thinning crowd, were Mr. and Mrs.

Brian Wilcox, whom she would forever and always call Cat and Willy. Cat and Willy had been lost, left behind with everybody else in Vienna when they all got on the train for Frankfurt and she waved good bye and got on with her life. Vienna -- all their kisses and good wishes washed over by time. Those powerful adolescent tears long dried and slowly vanished away, until finally there weren't even Christmas cards to betray their existence. She lifted her glass into the night and wondered what she was going to do.

"Denny? Denny Braithwaite?"
She looked up into the middle-aged face of what used to be Karen Ellis. It wasn't real. It was uncanny. The eyes, mouth, curve of the chin, even the hairstyle were the same, just older. It was like looking at a computer enhancement. Then it was real. The two second vertigo jolt from her heart, her muscles flash-drained and spongy.

"My God, girl. You haven't changed a bit!" Karen spoke.

She steadied herself with the table.

Karen Ellis used to be a better liar.

"Brian!   Brian!   Look, it's Denise.   You remember Denise."

Brian was a beefy version of something familiar until he got into the light and then she could clearly see it was Brian – Wilcox -- Willy, thicker, more ponderous, wearing a golf shirt and cargo shorts. Golf shirt and cargo shorts? She almost laughed, and then she did laugh, covering it with a quick "Wow, what are you two doing here?"

"What are we doing here? What are you doing here?"

"I live here. Just there, actually." She pointed vaguely into the sky.

"We thought you were in Berlin. Your mother said you were in Berlin."

"I have an apartment there too, so I divide my time …"

Karen just kept talking, half bent over the table, crowding against her, Brian's three-button green shirt looming awkwardly over her shoulder. So she stood up. Karen straightened, abruptly cutting herself off in mid sentence.

"Are you here for dinner?"

She nodded dumbly, looking over her shoulder for confirmation.

"Yeah, we were just really – uh -- kinda lookin' for a place," she said.

Brian still hadn't said a word, and it didn't like look he was going to in the near future.

"Come, sit down. Join me, please. What a coincidence!" she said, waving her hand expansively at the table.

There was a definite hesitation, uncomfortable seconds where they didn't know what to do. Desperately trying to read each others' minds, they were each one searching for a way out. Did they have other plans? Karen half stepped back against her husband. Were they waiting for someone? Brian shuffled sideways, giving his wife room. Were they having a fight? Then she knew, absolutely knew; she could read it in their faces. They hadn't told each other. They'd never talked about it. Even after all these years, they'd never gotten together and compared notes. And now, out of nowhere, they were scared stupid that she was going to do it for them.

"Really! Come! I insist.' She stuck her hand in the air and snapped her fingers extravagantly, taking control of the situation. They seemed impressed.

"I'll have Marco set two extra places. Oh, it's so great to see you guys again." She stepped around the table and pulled Cat forward and hugged her. She half kissed her quickly on both cheeks and let her go. There was more of Cat than she remembered, but at least she didn't stiffen or go soft in her arms. Brian was different. He was tense to the touch, but he held onto her for a minor second longer than necessary, tilting his face away from her lips. She slid away from him, indicating the table.

"You must try the vongolese." She said.

They did, and between that, bruscetta, two bottles of Chianti, cheese and finally tiramisu, she heard twenty years of the Brian and Karen story. They'd gotten married in college. They had two teenage daughters, Melissa and Sarah, allegedly left in a hotel room. This was their first trip back to Europe. And that the trip itself was all part of a much bigger adventure. Mr. Marshall's History and Civics class of Nathan Hale High School was coming back to Europe, Paris particularly, to recapture their youth, brag, gloat, apologize, see what had happened to who and generally realign the pecking order.

"I'm surprised you didn't know. The committee sent you the information sheets, I'm sure. I know they got the address from your mother. I talked to her just before we left. That's how come we thought you were in Berlin. I didn't have much to do with it, actually, just helping out. It's mostly Wendy and Clinton. They asked me to get involved, but I just didn't have time. You know, the girls are in high school now, and there's my job."

Karen spent most of the actual meal babbling on as though it was a nervous twitch. It wasn't until the second bottle of wine that she settled down and they could all talk together. Not that Denise did much talking, but in a lot of listening, they filled in most of the pieces for her. It wasn't very interesting, really. Struggling apartment, small house, one child, bigger house, assorted cars and better jobs, another child -- indicated as an accident -- a still bigger house, and so forth and so on. But looking through it all, past the insurance, the new shingles and the dance lessons, they hadn't changed. She could see it in them, the way they laughed, or smiled, they way they told their stories, their gestures. They might call themselves Brian and Karen, but underneath the dark washable tourist green, they were still Cat and Willy.

She ordered limoncello and coffee.

"Do you think they have decaf?"

They didn't, but they said they did, and they all drank it anyway. And as the evening turned into night, she found herself liking them. She had loved them so dearly so separately as a child, it was good to like them now. Karen -- Cat -- her high school best friend forever, who sat next to her in English, played tennis and volleyball, knew all the answers and cried so hard when she broke her wrist and even harder when Jimmy Dickenson broke her heart. And Brian -- Willy, the last official Hall Monitor, too serious to play football. He was saving his money for college, not a car. She had called him Wilcox since grade school, and after they started sleeping together, it seemed only natural to shorten it to Willy, Willy Boy, a private joke. They were nice people. But later, at the door, she just couldn't help herself.

"Look, you're going to be here for a couple more days. Why don't I take a day or two off work and show you the real Rome?"

"Oh, no! Really, we'll be fine."

"Thanks, but we couldn't impose."

They spoke almost simultaneously.

"It's no problem. Besides, I'd love to meet the children. And you haven't told me anything about Wendy's plans for Paris. I should at least know where everybody's going to be. Who knows? I might even go."

It was probably only the wine, but she could feel them subside, acquiesce; it was a good word, their objections lifeless and lame. Their real life, the last twenty years, put on hold by the secrets of power they didn't understand

"Great, I'll pick you up at your hotel -- say 10ish -- and we'll run around like fools and see the city. It'll be just like the old days."

On her twinkle-light balcony, she drained her glass. "I'll figure it out in the morning," she thought and went off to bed.

The European spring had been brilliant, unplanned to the last mishap. Twenty-three kids from Mr. Marshall's History and Civics Class, off to conquer Europe. They had saved their pennies all year and a month before graduation had set out to boldly go where no eighteen year old had probably ever gone before. In fact, given the complete lack of planning and supervision, it hadn't gone too badly. They lost Ms. Reynolds and most of their luggage in London, missed any number of buses and trains, had four cases of food poisoning, one serious illness, two and a half arrests and a traffic accident. They lost tickets, they lost passports, a couple of times they were robbed and Jerry Painter got stabbed in Seville. There was one serious drug overdose (the rest were minor), six or seven declarations of undying love, at least two fistfights, somewhere around nine cases of post-virginal depression, one pregnancy and one defection. And that didn't include all the minor scrapes, bumps, arguments, tears and swearing. Stranded in Amsterdam, the bus happily chugging away without them, Mr. Marshal quietly gave up and took to drink and so, by the time they got lost in Rhiems, Mr. Marshal's friend Call-Me-Janet was spending her days clucking and Wendy Sherwood and her clique were running the show. It became Lord of the Flies with museums.

Yet the spring had indeed been brilliant. Everything was new and they were immortal, fearless gods and goddesses with bright big eyes and smooth skin. They knew everything, saw everything, tasted, smelled and felt everything. And Europe did its best to help them. Hot humid days, sticky to the touch, and nights dark and silky, shivering with promises. Unknown narrow streets shadowed in grey stone and smooth cool white marble. Holy chanting churches and painted pagan rituals. Strong spices, sweet fruit, dark eyes and lisping vowels. Their families and bedtimes and televisions oceans away, they reverted to adolescent savagery. They ran mad over the cobblestones, each catastrophe binding them closer together, until they became a primitive tribe. Teenage warriors marauding across the continent, looting with their senses and brawling with their emotions. Their passions bubbling alive, their nerves high and open, dripping with hormones, they fought and danced, laughed, sang, kissed and hated. Then they all sobered up and went home. All of them -- except Denise.

The next morning Denise woke up early. She brought her coffee out to the cool of the balcony and watered her plants. It was going to be a hot day, and she wondered what to wear. Amsterdam had been hot, brilliant-sunshine warm, not like Paris, close and muggy and irritable. It had rained in Paris and the group couldn't get away from each other. The hotel smelled of onions and old pee. Karen and Denise, fighting with Wendy and flung out into the streets. Long overcast walks and chilly dingy cafés and the crying cold midnight at Jim Morrison's grave. She stopped it there. That was ahead of it; Amsterdam was first. Nothing she remembered could remember Amsterdam. Jerry Painter slumped over his shoes, drooling. Tammy Tamara dancing in the streets with the German boys. No, it was all blind stoned and stumbling on black beer and harsh sweet smoke and the night she pulled Wilcox -- he was still Wilcox then -- through the hot neon streets, kissing and touching and watching, until they couldn't stand it anymore. In the hard shadows of some brick broken alley they groped and grabbed and slipped down the stones like thickening oil, twisting and pulling at their clothes until they were on the ground. Then, barely on top of her, their tightened adolescent energies simply overflowed against each other. That she remembered, and moved slightly in her chair: the weight of him on her. She teased him unquenchably, holding herself to him, provoking and promising, watching the want of her in his eyes. And he so loved her, like a warm sleepy puppy. He wrote her sweet notes and poetry. She still had them -- somewhere. He opened doors for her and gave her advice, secretly planning his – uh -- their future. And she loved him back, but not that way. She knew that, even at the time. She loved him because he was nice, because he loved her, because unconsciously he taught her how to be adored, how to be enjoyed, and how to use power -- not hers -- she already knew that -- his. The male power of him moving through a crowd so she could see, dominating the background so she could win arguments. The tall shoulders beside her that made it easier to wait on a corner or walk at midnight or swear at cab drivers. And she showed him the power of the secret, more intimate than desire or sex or love itself. The secret shares a single soul so holy you dare not speak its name. It entangles and binds two people together so completely that forever, they are never alone in the world again. But that was later; that was Paris. She finished her coffee and set the cup down.

"Spanish blue dress, red purse and sandals," she thought, "Generic Italian: simple, cool and sexy." The dress touched in the right places but didn't cling, and the sandals had enough heel to tighten her calves, but she could still walk easily.

She stroked her shin and decided against another cup of coffee.

"And not too flamboyant" she thought. After all, she didn't want to scare anybody. But then she needed a hat, wide brim with a red band, to match the shoes. That was for Cat.

The family was waiting for her, assembled in the lobby of the hotel. They were dressed in 21st Century Tourist and looked just about as happy. For a surprising instant she felt bad about pushing them around the night before, but then... She shrugged and met the girls. Obviously coerced and threatened into their best behavior, they were too old to be travelling with the parents but too young to be on their own. Well, not so young really. Not much younger than she and Cat had been.

"Come, girls," she said. "Young ladies simply cannot walk around Rome without sunglasses. It just isn't done."

Out on the street, she found a vendor who knew a good thing when he saw it. He raised the price and flirted unmercifully. And so she danced and laughed and flirted back, translating his English and correcting their Italian. It set the tone for the day as they wandered in a great circle north that would eventually take them to Keats and the Spanish Steps. She played with the children to show the parents she was harmless. Treating them like friends, she became a benevolent older woman, fascinated by their youth. She laughed and talked and listened to their stories and she bought them things: junk jewelry and sweet sodas. At lunch, she offered them wine, slowly enough for Brian to smile and intervene. Even Cat relaxed a little. It was a nice day together.

Somewhere in the late afternoon, she and Brian ended up dragging behind the girls and their mother, slowly strolling across the brilliant sun-green Borghese Gardens. After some serious long pauses and a couple of wooden 'How ya beens?' Brian stopped and turned slightly towards her, making her stop with him.

"I would have come back, you know," he said. "I meant to. I wanted to, but..."

"I know," she said sympathetically, shaking her head and stepping forward. "Life has a way..."

She rolled her hand dismissively and they fell into step again.

"We didn't exactly keep in touch," she said finally.

"No, but it was – I don't know – you know – we were -- we weren't just kids – we said…"

She stopped him there.

"We said a lot of things that spring. And," she added slyly, "did a few things besides."

She watched him blush. This was better. She didn't want him uncomfortable, sorrowful, apologetic. It was a beautiful day, and she was having fun. And she wanted him to have fun too, enjoy her company the way he used to. Think well of her, and remember it all fondly. No. Actually no, that wasn't it, at all. She wanted him to want her. She was softly blowing on twenty-year-old embers so they would warm, heat and glow. So he would think of her and remember and wonder what would have, what might have, been. Tonight, let him lie in bed and feel her, see her walking now in the sunshine and remember the way her body fit with his, and think about now. How would it feel, now? And though she wondered if it touched on the edges of cruel, she thought it didn't and he would indeed remember it all fondly. And besides, it was fun, walking, matching his step, swinging her hat in her hand.

"What did you do after you left us?" he said. "I remember your parents: God, were they some pissed at Marshall! He got fired, you know."

"Yeah, I heard. The parents flew over here right away. What a hell of a mess that was, let me tell you," she laughed, remembering it. "I imagine I was all over town, too."

"Nah, not really," he said. "Well, yeah, kinda. Jerry went to California and Clint and Wendy got married real quick. So you were it. You know how the rumor mill works."

"No, I was safely on this side of the Atlantic."

"Hey!" she shouted across the park to the girls, "Gelato!"

"There!" she pointed, but the girls came back to them, the younger one running ahead of her sister.

"See that hedge where your mother is? Right behind it, up the little hill there's an ice cream stand. Bring us something."

She reached into her purse.

"What do you want?"

"Something fattening," she said, pointing her face at the girl and puffing up her cheeks with air.

"Dad?"

"Come on, Dad," Denise said, "Come on, pleassse. My treat." She paused just long enough to hand the girl money and then… "Go, go, go," she clapped her hands, "Quick before he changes his mind."

The girl obediently ran back to her sister.

"Come, sit," Denise said, dropping her hat and purse on the ground. "They're beautiful girls."

She pulled the hem of her dress slightly higher and sat on her hip tucking her legs behind

13

her. Brian stood over her for a second then sat down stiffly, knees bent, back straight.

"They take after their mother."

She laughed, "If I know you, Willy Boy, Karen didn't do all the work."

He blushed again, uncomfortable.

"Aw, come on. Lighten up," she said, hinting at irritation. "Remember me?"

He looked pained.

"It's just hard – you know – I really don't know what to say. All these years and everything... I don't want you to think..."

She pushed her body forward and rolled onto her stomach, bending her knees and crossing her ankles in the air. He stopped talking. She leaned up on one elbow, offering him a glimpse down the front of her dress. But then she looked over at him, arms wrapped around his knees, eyes open into the sun, hoping for his family to come back. This was still her Willy Boy. He had loved her, trusting and warm, and had traveled with her, the long distance, that spring, from what was girl to what would become woman. He deserved better than this, trapped and teased, still trying his best.

"Hall Monitor to the end," she thought and sat up.

"Leave it, Brian. We were kids," she said. "We had a hell of a good time. I did, anyway."

He turned his face back to her.

"But..."

"But, nothing!"

"But at the end it was all – just – left. You never told me anything. We're all getting on the train, and then suddenly you're not. Everybody was there and I couldn't say anything, tell you anything. Ya, Ya just left. Christ! Marshall didn't even know you were gone 'til we got to the border. What was I supposed to do?"

"You guys would have talked me out of it," she said, remembering those feelings for real. "And I just couldn't go back. God, I would have been trapped. I'd have ended up...Christ..."

She shivered.

"Like me and Karen?" he said.

"No, that's not what I meant," she said quickly, although even that had crossed her mind.

He shrugged. "Maybe, but that doesn't mean I haven't thought about it. What would have been, could have been. I've thought about it a lot. What if I'd come back to get you? What then? There's no problems or anything." He waved his hand vaguely, "We're alright, the girls are great and Karen's really special, but you know, you wonder sometimes."

"I know," she said, understanding him. "What about Karen?"

"Aw, I don't know. You guys were really close. She told me one time, like, when we first got home, that she'd never have another best friend. When you left... she like... she cried the whole way on the train." He was shaking his head. "We never really talked about it. We did at first, a little, but, after, like you know, later, you guys were such good friends I just... I just never..."

Yes, this was still her Willy Boy. No length of years could diminish that. She wanted to be good to him, for him and for Cat.

"Yeah, I know," she said, "I understand."

"At first, it didn't matter. Then things just started happening and…. it's just complicated. It would be…"

"Hey," she said, stopping him, "It was ours. That's it. Full stop. We went through that whole time, just you and me. I've always thought of it that way – us -- just us. Nobody knows. Nobody needs to know."

"Yeah, but I want to explain it. I wish I had more time." He looked anxiously into the park. "God, we never had enough time."

"As I remember that wasn't such a big problem in the old days."

He looked at her shyly.

"You didn't see me complaining."

Finally, he smiled.

"I just want you to know I didn't forget you Den. I've never forgotten you. I remember us so much but… now… it's… "

She leaned her cheek into her open hand and smiled sideways at him like somebody's coy mistress.

"Your secrets are safe with me, Wilcox," she said, and they understood each other again.

"Can I ask?"

She shrugged.

"Do you have someone?"

"Yeah, kinda. I've got a business partner. He and I hook up a couple of times a year. We connect -- food, fashion, ideas, evenings in the moonlight -- that sort of thing."

"Is it alright?" He put his hands open in front of him.

"Umhum," she said, nodding slowly and looking directly at him.

There was a small pause and then she said. "Remember Rome the first time? We came through here." She pointed at the ground

"You and me?"

"No, the whole gang. Remember? We were supposed to go to the gallery, but the tickets got all screwed up. They were for the day before or something, and you guys bought all that beer."

"Yeah, down there in the trees. And you and Karen got lost trying to find the bathroom."

"We didn't get lost."

"You were gone for like three hours. It was dark when you got back!"

Now they could play. He was safe and they could be friends. So they talked for a moment and laughed as the family came back, melted and sticky. It was good and it was good for him. The way it should be.

"You shouldn't have, really," Karen said, holding the dripping gelato out over the grass. "First the sunglasses, the earrings, then lunch, then… Damn."

"This mess?' Denise answered, handing her a napkin.

"Ms Braithwaite, are you our aunt or something?"

"Call me Dene." She pronounced it in the French way. "Everybody does. No, I'm not your aunt or even something." And just seeing Cat casually like this, she decided. "But I have permission from your Dad to spoil you two rotten for one more day. So, tomorrow, we're going shopping for clothes, and you can have whatever you want. Then I'm going to take your mother out and we're going to eat mountains of garlic and chocolate and," she put her hands out to indicate the size, "and drink buckets of cheap red wine."

"No, Denny, you can't...."

"Sure, I can. It's my town, my shop, my clothes. I can do what I want. Hot Italian Street Wear, girls!"

"No, I've got tons to do. I have to pack and get ready and..."

"Who said you're coming? Shopping? I don't think so. But tomorrow night, Dad and these two can handle the packing, and you and I are on the town. Right, girls? Whadda you say? Mom deserves a night out, doesn't she?" She knew Willy was on her side now, and the girls were "Yah, Mom!" And besides, what was she going to say? No?

Quite simply, Cat was trapped, and both women knew it.

Later, when it was all over, Denise sat alone on her balcony. The soft night below paused, occasional white velvet lights gliding out of the darkness and vanishing away again, like homeless drifting spirits. In all, it was quiet and empty. The peaceful night she always enjoyed. There was nothing to do now. Pick up the wineglasses, go in, turn off the lights and go to bed. Tomorrow the family would leave, sliding away from her on the train to the airport. Come and gone and over. Would she go to Paris? No. It was too precious to her to give away to that crowd. But she would go to the train, smile and wave and hug them away. She would go. She'd promised.

The evening had begun wary and anxious. Cat chattering away on the edge of her chair. Complimenting the food, the décor, Rome itself and some guy she mistook for a waiter. Giving Denise more of the same, her clothes, her style. Until finally, unable to watch the minutes rolling away, Denise broke it, dropping her fork loudly into her plate.

"For Christ's sake, Cat. I'm not going to tell him."

"I know," she said, stopping everything and putting her hands together in a prayer, "I wasn't sure, at first. God, I didn't know what to think. It was such a shock, seeing you. I thought you were in Berlin."

"Normally, I am. I usually don't get back here until the autumn show, but we had some problems. Fate."

Cat took a deep breath.

"Look, I don't want anything, or need anything," Denise said, "I just want a pleasant evening. I haven't seen you in twenty years. I missed you."

"I don't know what to say to you."

"Well, for starters, how come your girls are Melissa and Sarah? What about Denise? Denise is a nice name."

"You always hated Denise. You said it made you sound like somebody's ancient aunt."

"That's not the point. It would have been a nice gesture," she said seriously.

Cat looked up and caught the fool lurking in Denise's eyes, and, for the first time in three months, three days and twenty years, they laughed together.

"See how easy it is?"

"I missed you too, Denny. I've been worrying and wondering what to do with you. What to say."

"Don't worry about it. Let's just have a good time. Your girls were brilliant today."

"Thank you so very much," Cat took a mock bow. "We had a fashion show. And we're probably going to have to buy another suitcase. All that stuff must have cost you a fortune."

"Not so much. I just think about all the birthdays and Christmases I missed. What did you guys do?"

There was a pause.

"Oh." Denise said, and they laughed together.

And that's how it was, a real reunion, just without memories. They talked across the surface of their lives, reviving the events they had missed in each other. They had known each other so much, so young, that they were intimate strangers.

There was no risk of any misunderstanding. They each knew what the other was, her very spirit, and they enjoyed that and so they lingered, unwilling to break the connection now that it had been reconnected. And it was actually Cat who first spoke about it all.

"Are you going to Paris?"

"I don't know, maybe."

"Don't think you have to stay away."

"I don't, but," her voice dragged a bit. "I don't know those people. I remember the names and what they were but... Although I wouldn't mind getting another crack at Wendy Sherwood and that crowd."

"It's Maxwell now, Mrs. Wendy Maxwell, but they haven't changed. Clinton's on the Parks Board. Dinner with the Governor, don't you know." Cat's voice spun with sarcasm.

"Oh, God! Insufferable."

"Yeah, pretty much."

"And I'd practically have to hold a press conference. All the gossipy bits are going to come out."

"Yeah, everybody's going to ask. You wouldn't believe the stories that are still going around."

Denise dropped her hand at the wrist.

"What are you going to tell them?"

She shrugged the question off. She simply didn't care. For her, Paris was a place she visited often and traveled to a couple of times a year. And she wanted to tell Cat that. Explain it. In fact, she wanted to tell Cat everything. The crappy jobs she'd had. The places she'd lived. The people she'd slept with. The things she'd done to get what she wanted. And all the rest too, but most of all the reason. How vividly she remembered the clinging cold in Paris. The ache of the overnight train to Marseilles. The always smells and sounds she carried with her; the stained wallpaper in the cheap room under the Alhambra, the naked grass of the Borghese on her back. The thick Vienna cream oozing out of her mouth and the throbbing burn descending and descending until she finally realized no quench would ever put it out. All of it, everything. How Père Lachaise still made her cry. Cat knew the what of it, the events, but maybe not the why -- maybe not the deep and solid why. But now, finally sitting close enough to tell her, Denise realized they only had these minutes, steady and unstoppable, and there wasn't going to be enough time. She didn't know what to do. For all her planning and control, she was powerless. The evening was going to end, and the train was going to leave, and there was nothing she could do about it. She reached over with both hands, and, for a long few seconds, she held Cat's hand between them.

"Come on," she said letting go, "I've got something to show you."

And maybe it was her look or her tone, or maybe just the night, but Cat didn't hesitate. They paid the bill and crossed the street. They went up in the elevator and Denise opened the door to her apartment. She moved out of the way and turned on the lights.

Across the room, dominating it, was a picture. It wasn't huge but big with texture and movement and that gave it prominence. It was a crisp sharp photograph of a young woman slightly turning to look back into the camera. The background, rushed past her in blurred lines of bold color, long streaks of speed that threatened to carry her away with them. She was beautifully young, her hair tucked back to frame her face and show the light on her throat, the bright shadows of her cheekbones and her mouth slight and subtle, just parted. The first revealing blossom of woman. But her eyes, full and vivid over her shoulder, were still child, open and questioning, searching beyond the camera. It was a fragile beauty, just caught before she turned back and was swallowed by the photo itself. She was not sad as much as lost, and not lost as much as forlorn.

"Oh, God!" Cat sagged into the doorway. "I can't do this, Denny," she said.

"I wanted you to know -- for sure. I wanted you to see."

She stepped forward and straightened Cat up by the shoulders, holding her at arm's length and talking directly to her.

"I have another one just like it in Berlin. It's why I didn't get on the train. Why I'm never going back. Because everything I'm ever going to have is right there."

In the deep end of the night, Denise swirled the last touch of wine into her glass. Cat had stayed and they had talked. And, cloaked in the shadows of the balcony, they re-told the promises they never should have made. Now Cat was gone and Denise knew, without looking, that it was already tomorrow, and there would still be every tomorrow. And she knew that, even when you believe in magic, have touched it and tasted it and held it in your hand, broken pieces of your life or what you love, don't mend. And the mistakes you make so young, no matter what they are, are etched in stone. But just for now, it was alright, and it wasn't a sin to be a coward or selfish or know what you want -- it just hurt.

In Rome, Via Cavour runs directly from the tourists to the ruins, but she loved the look of the street at night, all patched together in the darkness.

------/\------

....Scars

The three scars were long and deep, cut into the floor in another century and now smooth and round with age. Idly she pushed her sandal off and followed the lines with her toes. They ran parallel and started close, spread slightly for an inch or two and then shallowed and died. Her toes splayed as they moved through the lines, and, near the end, had to grip to hold the form. The grooves were wide enough to hold her comfortably and she lingered there in their ruts.

The drinks were tall and sweaty. Their sides dripped and ran, their white water puddles made high top pearls on the dark wooden table. It was only the other two customers that kept her from licking the sides of her glass.

They had walked all morning through the lower town. It had been cool and touristy, with people from the market laughing and performing for them. They had bought fruit, the huge fresh kind that only comes in the tropics, and tried stupidly to get the woman to wash it for them.

Then they had started up the long steep streets that led to the old town. The morning faded, and the fierce heat afternoon found them wandering over the stones of the last century, and it made them stop to argue about washing the fruit which she ate anyway. It was rich and pulpy and the sticky juice ran down her face and up her arms, leaving dirty streaks. And his tone was, "You'll be sorry!" But she didn't care because the juice was cool and she was thirsty, more thirsty than she had even been. And there was more, the deep purple colors hanging in the string bag he carried. But she didn't ask; he was angry anyway. And they continued up away from the sea and into the hot afternoon.

And now she was cradled in the scars underneath the table, feeling them with her large middle toe, stroking the rounded sides and pausing in their length. It was cooler here, not much, but the thick dark walls and the deep shadows helped. And the afternoon which had covered them and collected in streaks where their clothing fit was waning, moving across the white sky, too late now to stalk them. But they were still quiet from the climb, their hair lank at the back of their necks, their clothes dry stained and their muscles languored and tired. So they sat, idling their drinks; he, reading the thumb-worn brochure from the counter and she, smoothing caresses out of three ancient scars.

She turned her drink in her hand, feeling the cool wet of it on the ends of her fingers and leaned forward and sucked at the straw, filling her mouth with the frothy liquid. He looked up.

"Don't drink so fast on an empty stomach. In this heat you'll get sick." he said.

She swallowed. She remembered hearing that from her father once but she thought he had been talking about horses.

"This was a slave market," he said, matter-of-factly.

Her toes stopped in the middle scar and she pulled her foot back under her chair.

"See?" he said, pointing the brochure at her, "A slave market."

She looked away across the thick sill, out into the gravel afternoon. The pebbles crunched under the tall heels of a woman walking just out of sight. She felt her through the soft of her footfalls that moved with a practiced space in sound and speed.

"High heels, on the gravel, in this weather?" she thought

"Just right here was for viewing and over there where the bar is was the prom...in...prom"

"Promenade," she corrected.

"Promenade," he repeated. "And they were kept out in the yard. Trooped from the ships just the way we came." He was obviously delighted with his discovery and was warming to it.

The woman came in through the tall open doors. Her dress was crisp orange, stiff and sharp, even in the heat. Her hat was full, with a trail of white ribbon that fell from the side. The shadow of it partially hid her face and forced her to hold her head a little too high. She stopped full on her feet then walked past them. She walked with the same measured step and sat down at a table across from them, so that she was in the shallow shadows. Her profile and her right shoulder were in their direct view. She took off her sunglasses and laid them on top of her gloves, white like her hat ribbon and her shoes.

"The owners lived upstairs, and this was the first building in the Americas to have running water."

The waitress walked by them, carrying a tray with a bright metal coffee service, a small decanter of amber liquid and two wide crystal glasses. She poured the coffee, added one spoon of sugar and stirred it. The woman nodded her head to thank her and the waitress turned to go back to the bar.

"Could we have another, please?"

"Remember you haven't eaten anything today except that fruit and that'll probably make you sick. It said in the brochure that you should wash everything thoroughly and avoid the local produce."

"Just one more won't kill us. Besides, it's too hot and I'm tired"

"Don't whine, Jen. Just remember what I told you. You'd hate to spoil everything by getting sick. Yes, miss. One more for each of us."

The woman sat turned slightly away from them. She reached back from her handbag with a cigarette and snapped a large, old-fashioned lighter. The flame briefly illuminated her face fully, and Jen saw that she was older than she had originally thought. Her body and carriage had been firm, her legs and arms round with female muscles. Her legs were crossed and her dress rode up on her thighs. She was toying with her shoe, half on her foot, pushing the heel back and forth with her toes. Yet her face was full and held the extra worry lines that made Jen think of her mother. The woman turned and caught Jen staring. Jen looked away but still saw the woman pull a thick lungful of smoke from the cigarette and exhale it as she now stared at Jen. She did this twice, while Jen, avoiding her eyes, finally became so embarrassed she reached for her purse.

"I have to go to the toilet," she said and stood up and turned and left the table.

She passed the waitress bringing their drinks and acknowledged her with a slight smile. They met between tables and had to turn their bodies to get by. They passed close enough for Jen to hear the rustle of fabric her thighs made when she walked and smell her perfume that touched her tongue for a second. It was exotic and old and tasted musty. Then she was gone and it was gone and the toilet was cool. The tiles were nearly cold on her feet. Her feet? She had forgotten her sandals under the table and had walked barefoot through the restaurant, bar, slave market. Her first inclination was to go back and she eyed the floor suspiciously from the inside of the door. Everything was white and bright and clean.

"No puddles," she thought. "And doors!"

She went to the first cubicle and shut the door. Her baggy walking shorts slid easily to the backs of her knees, but her panties were damp and rolled down the outside of her thighs. The middle clung to the hair and formed a bright shield halfway down. The walls were clean and white with no trace of leftover graffiti, what a Ladies Room is supposed to be. She reached and unrolled the paper, wadding it up and remembering to wipe down as the doctor had told her, not up as her mother had taught her. She checked for color and stood up, unrolling her panties and pulling up her baggy shorts. She twisted and picked her clothes into place and was about to flush when the outside door opened and someone came in. She stood nervously still, trying to control even the sound of her breathing, waiting for a cubicle door to close, so she could leave. But none did, and even though she didn't want to meet the woman in orange in the female privacy of a toilet, she flushed and opened the door.

    It was the waitress, preening in front of the mirror, whipping at her long cheekbones with the stubby hairs of a makeup brush, her hands expertly smoothing the deep shade and avoiding the intricate dangle of her earrings. She bit at her lips to puff the color and Jen automatically bit at her own. Their reflected eyes met in the mirror and Jen stepped forward, pulling her fingers through her hair, adding some shape to the lank strands.

    "You are still warm here, Mrs," the waitress said.

    Jen smiled, "I'm not used to the heat. We don't get heat like this at home."

    "No, Mrs."

Mrs. seemed odd to Jen. Nobody called her Mrs. anything -- ever -- and she never thought of herself as Mrs. She ran water over her hands. It felt cold. She didn't like Mrs. Jen looked up sideways at the waitress again. She was well-done, a beauty. "But obviously older than me," Jen thought. Then she looked at herself in the mirror: her hair hung, she had no makeup and her face showed the greasy remains of the sunscreen she had put on that morning. Her earrings were small, colorless spots. Her lips looked washed, tired and washed.

The waitress put away her stubby brush and watched the younger woman for a second. She took a squat copper bottle from her bag.

"Sometimes, Mrs., it's better to feel better," she said.

Jen straightened and turned away from the mirror.

"Here. Let me show you."

The waitress reached around Jen's neck and into her hair. Her fingers spread and pushed the hair up and away from her neck. Jen stiffened, but the woman pushed further, drawing even the tiny guard hairs up and away from Jen's skin. Jen felt her pulse rising and beating against the heel of the woman's hand as it firmly held her head and her hair. Her breath caught.

"Don't call me Mrs.," she said, "Please," as her breath escaped.

The waitress reached up with her free hand and turned the copper bottle over Jen's exposed neck. Three liquid drops felt like pearls as they slid from the bottle and touched her skin. They were cool and old and musty and spreading, seeking the ruffles of each pore that drank at them. The woman smiled up at Jen as the liquid dissolved or evaporated or soaked in. Jen felt the the woman's fingertips and the drag of her nails as she released her hair and worked the last of the perfume into the hollow of her neck where the small hairs were.

"Women sometimes need pleasant things when they are warm. It feels better now?"

"Yes" Jen said, and it did. She felt cool and smooth. The dry skim added to her body and spread out into her shoulders. The taste cleared her head. It was the same scent as when the two women had passed in the restaurant. The drag was gone. She felt stronger, more, even exotic.

Jen turned back to the mirror and ran water over her hands. She scooped handfuls onto her face and rubbed the sunscreen traces away. The water wasn't even cool, but it felt good. She took her hands and ran them through her hair, plumping it. They strayed to where the waitress had touched and her fingers lingered where hers had been, where the drops had fallen. Jen dragged them away and touched them to her lips. The taste was the same, unfaded. She lifted her head to say thank you and caught the edge of a reflection leaving the washroom. Her face was already dry.

The restaurant room had changed. Had she been in the washroom that long? The shadows were bigger, longer. And there were more people, at least a dozen. Jen looked for the waitress and found she was already busy, so she made a wide circle to her table, feeling the smooth glossy wood on the bottoms of her feet. She slid the pads of her feet against the wood, nearly skating across the floor, gliding to her table, concentrating on the feel of the wood, the spaces in the planks, the small sucking sound her steps made.

"Better than the click of high heels," she thought and looked up to find her table. The woman in orange was standing over Neil, listening intently to him. She stood angled over the chair on his left side. She leaned on it heavily. Her breasts were tucked between her arms and pushed out under his head. Jen watched as Neil's eyes drooped from the woman's face to the long 'Y' of her cleavage and shyly back to her face again. Jen knew the woman knew she was there, but she dropped her purse on the table anyway, scraped her chair back and bent down to retrieve her sandals. On her hands and knees she crawled under the table. From below, the woman's legs seemed longer and her high heels made the calf muscles tight, almost powerful. The sharp hem of her dress cut the hint of the line of her upper leg.

"She must shave every day." Jen thought and hooked her sandals towards her. They slid over, revealing the three long scars in the floor, and Jen automatically touched at them with her fingers. The fit was perfect. The measure of the length and the space between. And the sides weren't rounded but puffy, humped as if they were swollen.

She got up quickly and showed off her sandals like a hunting trophy to explain her behaviour, then dropped them and sat down. Neil looked at her defiantly. He had been looking at another woman's breasts but she had left him alone and so it was somehow her fault, and besides it was alright to look at breasts anyway. But all he could say was, "Where have you been, dear?"

Before she could answer that she'd had to pee (it always bothered Neil when she talked that way in public) the woman broke in.

"Your Neil has been telling me the history of this place. It was a slave market. But he has forgotten his manners and didn't invite me to sit. My name is Telia, and you are Jennifer."

The "t's" were on the front of her teeth, the pronunciation was firm and from the beginning of her mouth, melodic and Caribbean. No need for Telia to say "pee"; Neil was looking uncomfortable enough for forgetting his manners and displeasing the woman.

"I'm sorry I..." he started to say, but Telia continued.

"Your hotel is not far from here, Jennifer, but it is a long walk. If you stay for the show, I will arrange a car. I will arrange a car anyway, but you must stay for the show. It's very naughty. You will be my guests for the..."

Neil interrupted rudely, "I'm sorry, but we can't stay." He was looking harassed, "And at home we don't have to invite people to sit; they just do it."

Telia straightened up and turned her head slightly. "You are a long way from home, Neil." she said finally

"Did you come for the show?" Jen asked. Her foot had found the three scars again, and she was instinctively stroking her toes through them. She reached for her drink. It had melted, blotting the coaster with liquid that soaked through the cardboard fabric. It stuck to the bottom of the glass when she lifted it. Jen avoided the straw, pushing it aside with her tongue, and drank deeply, pulling her upper lip back from her teeth to strain the ice. She set the glass down, touching the coaster to the table first to break the vacuum. It came off the glass with a small, wet sound. She set the glass down on the table, rubbing it into one of the high puddles that had formed. Now her toes rested easily in the scars, only the middle one trembling slightly.

"No, I am waiting for someone. A new employee," Telia said, making a slight gesture in the air with her right hand.

Jen drank again.

"A new hostess," Telia said.

Jen slightly watched the recognition spread over Neil's face, even though she kept her eyes on Telia. She knew he had been flirting, showing off his local knowledge for the attractive woman who had approached him in a bar. Talking to her with authority. The waitress Jen had met in the washroom came to the table.

"Louise, these nice people are my guests this evening. And they will be using my car later. Have it brought around."

"Really, we can't stay."

"I'd like another drink, please, Louise."

"Jen, we have to go."

"I will talk with you later. Unfortunately, I have to work now."

"Really, ma'am, we..."

"'Telia,' Neil, please. If you need anything, Louise."

"Thank you, Louise." Jen said, trailing her right hand under her hair to the back of her neck.

"And you, sir?" Louise said.

"No, no, thank you. Look, it's awfully nice of you, but really. It's starting to get late and we have a big day tomorrow."

"We will talk later. I really have work to do," Telia said, dismissing herself.

She returned to her table and sat down, turning ever-so-slightly away from them. The big lighter flashed and she cupped the flame in her hand, holding it for a second against her cigarette. From Jen's angle, it appeared as if she was holding the fire to her face. Then the flare died and Jen noticed the room had gotten quite dark, the shadows were bolder and the tiny lights enclosed and futile. The long tropical afternoon only lingered, useless and forceless, unable to defy the inevitable twilight.

"Where did you go? I've never been able to understand why it takes women so long in the toilet. And that woman cornered me. I couldn't very well tell her to leave."

The room was darker and much more attractive. It was thick with glossy illuminated wood. The bar was in the right corner, shiny with light and glass; crystal columns that reflected on the dark tables, and in the faces and the eyes of the people. There were even more people now, arranged around the dark tables, their faces lit by single candles, or left as silhouettes in the larger darkness. Where had the light gone? Jen looked forward through the open window. There was still light outside, hampered by the gathering twilight but still clear.

"Why didn't you tell me that woman worked here? I was telling her all about it: who we were, where we were staying, and, of course, everything about this place; just like I knew what I was talking about, and all the time she knew. I feel like a complete fool. What took you so long? Where did you go, anyway?"

Jen looked down from the open window. Sitting in front of the light, Neil's features were indistinct and dissolving into shadows.

"I had to pee," she said.

"Oh, Jen! Look, I'm tired and dirty. I just want to go back to the hotel and clean up. I'll stay for a little while, but come on! I walked all over today."

The ceiling was high, lost in the upper reaches of the walls. Jen turned her chair so she could find it, following the blunt staircase that rose from the expanse of pale smooth floor that she had skated over. The wood of the floor was light and long, spreading from the bar until it stopped at the staircase that ran, quick and large, up from nowhere. It hung on the wall and followed it, suspended, hanging from the darkness and disappearing into it. The room, the tables, the people: all seemed to flow towards the long floor. Enclosed by the abrupt, shiny crystal of the bar, and the sudden rise of the stairs, it was backed by the black, wet wall. It was the focus.

"I don't know why we ever came in here in the first place. You were tired or thirsty or something. You've been difficult all day. First it was the fruit, then you had too much to drink, then ganging up on me with those other two women. That was just too much. I don't want to be her guest; I don't want to have her car; I don't want anything, right now."

Neil's left hand emphasized his words, crossing over the table in front of him, with the palm down. The fingers spread out towards her. A different girl came with Jen's drink. Jen reached up and plucked it off her tray.

"Thank you," she said.

"And you, sir?" the girl asked.

"Nothing. I don't want anything."

Jen took a small taste of it through the straw and set the glass down. She turned her chair back, directly facing Neil. She couldn't really see his face at all, anymore; couldn't see if he was angry or sad, disappointed or cruel. She watched the place where his face used to be, and, from the edge of her eye, saw the girl sitting with Telia. She was small, small enough for a man to hold. She wore dark clothes with bright white ruffles at her throat and her hands. Her hair lay over her back. Her earrings touched the light; her gloves were small; her shoes tied at the ankles. Jen saw Telia reach across and hold the girl's wrist. She watched as

Telia took the girl's glove off, each finger pulled out and away, as if it was her own hand. She examined the girl who dipped her fingers obediently. Jen moved her foot away from the scars on the floor. They were warm and moist from the warmth of her foot. She trailed the moisture with her toe as she pushed her sandals toward her chair.

"I'd like to stay for a while," she said.

There was no sound from the shape that was Neil. And there was no silence in the room to hear if he was breathing.

"You've had too much to drink," he said, "And I think we better go." His voice was sullen, deep after the high-pitched sounds he had been making.

"No," she said

She stood up and gathered her purse and her drink together, balancing them in one hand. She bent and lifted her sandals by the ankle straps, holding them firmly. The scars looked deep in the dim light and dark wood, deeper than she'd realized. She stood waiting, feeling the arm of the chair resting on the back of her leg. Neil didn't move, didn't speak.

"I'll meet you back at the hotel," she said.

"What brought all this on?"

She felt awkward standing there over him, balancing her purse and her drink, trying to think of something to say. She couldn't think of anything. She couldn't even see him. She turned her head into the darkness, expecting something, then walked the few quiet steps to Telia's table.

She placed her drink and her purse on the table, sat down and dropped her sandals on the floor.

"You've decided to stay for the show. Good. Jennifer, this is our new girl, Mary. Mary, this is our Jennifer. She's a long way from home, so we must make her feel especially welcome. Oh yes, we must. It will be just us. Girls' night out."

Mary touched the back of Jennifer's hand. Jennifer smiled and sipped her drink. Her foot was already searching under the table for scars.

------/\------

....The Ballad of Lisa and Lacey

Lacey was not a lesbian. In fact, after all these years, she wasn't even bi-curious. She considered herself a realist. She had a degree in Business Admin, and had worked for the same mega-multinational coffee company for so long she was on the day shift. She still told her friends she was turning irony into a career. She lived without frills in a three story walk-up in what was rapidly becoming a trendy neighborhood. Her real name was Lucinda, but a boyfriend from her freshman year had called her Lacey (after her man-catcher underwear) and the name had stuck. She had two discreet tattoos, but aside from that and her fingerprints, she could have been any woman looking 30 in the face and wondering "Where'd the time go?" But Lacey, as far as Lacey knew, was unique, because every year, regular as May the first, she packed two expensive suitcases and went on vacation -- with Lisa.

Lisa was a secret that had started one sharp rain April evening, nearly a decade earlier, when the woman who was weeping spilled her coffee. The neighbourhood wasn't trending then, and the high-heeled woman was out of place. Lacey, bored beyond relief, took pity on her and strolled over with a moist cloth to offer damage control, and even though she didn't know it at the time, it was love at first wipe.

That was the beginning. A random gesture that stretched into three more days. On the second night, over a very late, after work, dinner Lisa explained that long distance wasn't the best ingredient for love, and she'd been unceremoniously dumped in favour of someone closer at hand. Her heart was torn but not broken. Lacey, after two too many glasses of wine, offered that love was indeed a bastard and that three years of university had left her with no one and nothing but debt and doubt and no way out. They toasted their equally maddening and mixed up lives and decided two survivors needed to survive. Later, in Lisa's hotel lobby, there was a fragile secular two cheek kiss and a promise of lunch.

The next day was an afternoon, wet with glistening streets from a sun-broken, spring rain morning.

"Do you have a passport?" Lisa said, angling her eyes down and out of the bright bleached cafe window.

Lacey had a passport, somewhere. It was left over from a less than successful Greek and Roman senior trip. She looked skyward trying to remember if it was still at the bottom of her sock drawer or had she put it with the income tax.

"Yeah."

"I know this might sound crazy but the thing is -- the reason I'm here," Lisa pointed down, "Is we were going to take a trip to Europe." There was a pause, "Obviously, we're not going to now, but I -- um -- I still have the tickets." There was another pause, "And the tour company says I can't get the money back."

Lisa held out her hands, empty and open. There was silence.

"Are you asking *me*? I-I-I can't afford something like that."

"No, no. It's all paid for. Flight, hotels, food, everything. It's all-inclusive, five star. All we have to do is show up at the airport."

"Wow!"

"Well?"

"No." Lacey took a breath, "No, I can't. I've got school. I've -- I've got a job. I've got ... I -- I can't."

"Why not? Paris, a cruise down the Rhone river, the Riviera, back to Paris for a couple of days and home. Two weeks. It's the chance of a lifetime."

It was. It was the chance of a lifetime.

"Tell them you're sick. Tell them your aunt died. Tell them *whatever*. Come on! I really don't want to go alone.

"Why -- why me? You must have friends," Lacey said, shaking her head.

"It's the day after tomorrow, and everybody I know is back home. And they've got kids and commitments and everything's all so complicated with them. This is just the sort of wild and crazy thing I need to do right now."

The sun slanted across the table, but it was slowly fading as more clouds moved into the sky. It darkened the room and closed them in together.

"We click, Lace. We're *simpatico*. Come on, please. It'll be fun."

And there on the afternoon edge of dark and light, Lacey knew it would be fun. It would be bright and dancing with sprinkling fairy lights and rippling silver water, and it would be like nothing she'd ever done before. Lacey looked across the table. It was almost time for her to go to work. She could see Lisa's face clearly, and it was friendly and open and warm, and she was smiling.

The next day was easy. There had been a few "what ifs" from the shadows the night before, but with her rent paid, $306.00 in the bank, a credit card (with not that much on it) and bankable parents, Lacey finally went to sleep -- with Lisa taking her picture in front of the Eiffel Tower. In the morning, she found her passport (sock drawer) and telephoned Lisa with all the details. They agreed to meet for dinner at Lisa's hotel. Then she telephoned work and killed off her grandmother (not the live one.) Tony, the assistant manager, who'd "accidently" brushed past her ass more than once, was really totally sorry and offered to talk if she needed to but could only give her a week off -- without pay. That didn't bother Lacey. It was only a part-time job, and she didn't really like it that much anyway. Besides, she had a feeling Tony would probably rehire her. Then she went out to the university and borrowed a suitcase from Shannon, who was really totally sorry as well and said she'd cover Lacey's classes for her -- just in case. At some point, she thought about telephoning the parents, but she just wasn't up for the trial by combat her mother would put her through. And she already had a pretty good idea what kind of mountain of grief they'd give her if this thing went bad. It wasn't worth it to start the process early. And that was that. It was that simple. By the time Lacey was back in her apartment, looking at the open, empty suitcase, she had disconnected herself. For the next two weeks, she could say and do -- and be -- whatever she wanted to be, including, as it turned out, Lisa's daughter.

That's what they decided to do, at dinner that evening, just in case anyone on the tour asked -- and, according to Lisa, somebody was *bound* to ask. Actually, it wasn't that big a stretch: the two women had similar colouring and hair, and anyway it was a lot easier to explain than "we met at a coffee shop three days ago."

They tried it out on the bright smile hotel server when he brought the bill, and he seemed particularly pleased that they'd confided in him -- after admitting that he thought they were sisters.

"I don't have a sister." Lisa said, after he'd gone.

"Neither do I."

Lacey laughed, "Brothers?"

"Brother," Lisa corrected.

Lacey held up three fingers.

"All older," she said.

"Oh, my God," Lisa said. "I have one and that's bad enough."

Lacey held up her wine glass and shook her head.

"You don't wanna know. But here's a toast to the sisters we never had."

Their glasses barely touched, and the high-pitched single *tink* was inaudible -- except to the two of them.

"And I want you to know, I promise to be the best daughter you never had."

Lisa drank at her wine, set it down and smiled.

"I have a daughter, Lace, and a son."

Lacey held the wine glass to her mouth to conceal her surprise.

"And they aren't very much younger than you are."

Lisa waited. Lacey set her glass down. She wasn't sure what her reaction should be. This changed things. It wasn't "just us girls" going on an adventure anymore. Lacey knew that Lisa was older but ... she had never suspected she was anybody's *mother*. Mothers and girls were different. Mothers didn't get dumped by bastard lovers; they got divorced. Mothers had things, possessions -- stuff. Things they had to worry about. Girls worried about whether or not their underwear matched. Mothers had *responsibilities*. But the big problem was mothers and girls weren't *equals*. Lacey picked up her glass again.

"I'm only 37, Lace." Lisa said anticipating the question, "I had Ben and Courtney when I was quite young."

"Where are they?"

Lacey sipped her wine and set it down.

"At home."

"What? How come -- uh?"

"Let me show you." Lisa picked her telephone out of her handbag. She tapped and swiped a few times and then handed it to Lacey.

"That's them at the airport when I left on Monday. Ben, Court and Bertram -- my husband." Lisa said, reaching her finger across to point.

"I don't understand. Who'd you have the fight with here on Tuesday, then?"

"That was something that hasn't been working out for a couple of years, but neither one of us knew how to end it. So we just conjured up a big fight and now it's over."

"So your *husband*?"

"No. Bert's safe at home," Lisa looked at her watch, "Probably just climbing into bed with his receptionist."

"Oh," Lacey said with some distaste.

"It's no sin. What do you think *I* was doing Monday night? We live in a very small town, Lacey. Everybody knows everybody. I just prefer to keep my marital lapses *away* from the local rumour mill; that's all. So every year, rather than have my particulars discussed around the local campfires, I take a *business*," Lisa made finger quotes in the air, "*trip* to Europe."

"And your husband knows?"

"He knows something."

"What about the kids?"

From the picture they obviously weren't *children*.

"They're both old enough to hear the gossip," Lisa shrugged, "That's why I try to be as discreet as possible."

"So why drag *me* along?"

"Spur of the moment. Like I said, we click, you and I. You're smart, witty. You're kind. You were kind to me. It feels right, Lace. I can *talk* to you. I just want to go and have fun for a couple of weeks. A 'just us girls' adventure."

Lacey drank the last of her wine. Oddly, she felt very sophisticated, just then.

Later, back in her apartment, Lacey looked at the open, empty suitcase, closed her eyes to think and the next thing she knew she was sitting in a cafe with a bottle of red wine and Lisa -- and the spring sunshine warm in her hands. At least, that's what she remembered -- even now what she remembered. Everything else was just waking up and sleeping and waking up again in the white noise confusion of airports and airplanes and jetlag and the foreign sounds of travel. It was Monday or something, in this movie, but nobody seemed to care. People were eating soup and smoking and making noises she'd never heard before. But it was *her* movie too, and Lisa was laughing in French and the waiter smiled at Lacey like a grandfather and poured both glasses full. She refocused her eyes and it suddenly occurred to her that the big church sitting next to her was Notre Dame -- from all the movies. But the river wasn't a movie: it was the Seine -- and the people were French, and that was Lisa, and she was Lacey, and for the first time in forever the world was pinch-me real again.

Lisa lifted her glass and touched it to Lacey's. Tink.

"Paris."

Lacey lifted her glass.

"Paris," she repeated.

After that, there was no beige-green apartment anymore, no fruit smell in the stairwell, no winter wet buses, no back-row bored lectures, no stand around coffee stained evenings -- no -- no anything. Those were all more than an ocean away and belonged to Lucy, a third year admin student with a plague of good intentions. She liked Lucy -- she really did -- but they barely knew each other. Lucy was Lucy -- somebody else. *She* was the girl Lisa called "Lace." And Lace spent her days wandering through centuries of tour-guided art and architecture, until, utterly overwhelmed by beauty, she and her mother had to stop and sit and try and make sense of where they'd been and what they'd seen. The first day, they rejoined the tour later in the evening, but after that they didn't. They went off by themselves to eat and drink and flirt with their laughable French. On the second night, they met a couple of unlikely lawyers who bought them blonde Belgium beer but gallantly made their goodbyes when Lace called Lisa *ma mère*. Luckily, nobody laughed -- until "*les avocats*" were gone. The next night, they followed detailed instructions to an around-the-corner subterranean club called *La Feé Verte* where they danced into the morning to ferocious Techno-Dutch DJ music and got lost going back to the hotel which was only three streets away. On the last night, they hired a taxi that drove them deep into the Paris night, twinkling with magic. He charged them outrageously but waited patiently at Sacré-Coeur and again while, starlit and sleepy, they had a last glass of wine in the empty shadows of Montparnasse. The next day, Lace and her mother left Paris, the two of them sleeping quietly behind their sunglasses, as the tour bus swayed its way to the Rhone Valley. Seeing the two women curled up together, nobody on the tour believed the mother and daughter story anymore.

Paris had been fun, but it was the river Lacey remembered. Later, Côte D'Azur was too noisy and crowded and dancing, and when they went back to Paris, it was too short, too sad, too stilted. So, it was the river, long and lazy, that Lacey saw when she closed her eyes. The gliding evening light turning into night. The world around them fading away into shadows and stars and shiny rippling fingers that trailed along beside them. And the two lines of endless water spreading out behind them like the silver wings of a great dark serpent, pushing them forward and swallowing their tracks. And they were together alone in the shallow darkness as if no one could ever find them there. So, in the late evening they took their coffee on deck, which was surprisingly cold, and talked until the steward suggested brandy (he always suggested brandy) and then brought them each a blanket so they could remain there in the huge, whispering night. Over the years, Lacey had rewoven those nights into a single thread, hopelessly knotted and twisted together, but for her it would always be Lisa. Elegant, not delicate, impossible to unravel with maybe a single beginning but certainly no perceivable end.

"When we get to the Riviera, let's dress up and go someplace expensive and eat caviar and drink champagne until dawn?"
"I'll unpack my finest blue jeans."
"I'm sure they have dress shops in Côte d'Azur, Lace." Lisa said, "I can see you in something slinky and black -- cut down to here. You can borrow my silver chain and... we'll do your nails and let's get your hair done?"
Lacey hadn't had her hair done since her aunt did it for her in middle school.
"I'm not a Barbie?"
Lisa paused and looked at Lacey.
"Of course not."
Lisa laughed. "I'm Barbie. You're Skipper."
"Skipper? Like from Gilligan's Island?"
"No, Skipper -- Barbie's little sister. Didn't you have Skipper?"

"No, I must have missed that. We were poor people. All I had was Barbie. I didn't even have a Ken."

"Poverty's a bitch," Lisa said, swirling the brandy glass in the palm of her hand.

"Why business?"

"I don't know," Lacey shrugged, "Seems like a good idea. There's lots of jobs."

"No, really? Business Administration? You're not a bean counter."

"Yeah, I am, actually. I -- uh -- I -- this might sound weird, but I just love economics. Don't laugh. It's cool. The thing is a degree in economics doesn't get you anywhere, so I thought I'd get *into* it, with something that pays the rent and see where it goes."

"Good idea, I guess, but you should do what you love."

Lacey couldn't help herself.

"Is that what you do?"

"Of course." Lisa spread her arms into the night.

"Okay, next year *you* can be Skipper. The mother-daughter thing hasn't really worked, has it?" Lisa said, lifting her glass.

"Next year?"

"Yeah, where do you want to go?"

"You're joking?"

"Not at all. Aren't you having fun?"

"Yeah, but..."

"You graduate next year. Let's take a month and go to Italy."

"Whoa, I'm a bit lost. I thought this was your annual romantic..." Lacey opened her eyes wide, gritted her teeth and frantically pushed her hands back and forth without touching.

"Well, I never did it *that* way, but okay."

"It's just..."

Lisa held up her hand and stopped Lacey.

"Look around you. You're in *France* -- on a boat -- floating down the Rhone, snuggly warm, drinking cognac by candlelight under twinkling stars. How much romantic do you *need*?"

"There was a scandal when I was in high school. You've never lived in a small town, Lace. Believe me, small towns *thrive* on scandal. Anyway, I got married very quickly. He was from an old family and I was from a rich one, so everybody was happy. Three years later, I was a miserable, bad housewife with two kids. My father was dead, my mother had a nervous breakdown, my brother was busy losing the family fortune and my husband decided he wanted to be a dentist."

"What did you do?"

"I broke his nose!"

"Oh, my God, Lis!" Lacey laughed out loud and put her hands to her face.

"I didn't mean to. It was i*nstinct*." Lisa set her glass down. "I was bending over, loading the dishwater, and he came up behind me and grabbed my ass. I had one of those Telfon pans in my hand, and I just turned around and let him have it.

Bam! Knocked him cold. There was blood everywhere. It was just a total disaster."

Lacey was still laughing.

"Anyway, Bert was really good about it. He told everybody he fell down the stairs."

Lisa picked up her glass and sipped the brandy.

"After that, we kinda had an arrangement. But it occurred to me that the only way out of the mess I was in was to quit being the dutiful daughter. So I got my mother to sign over her shares in the company, and I booted my brother out."

"Wow!" Lacey was still half laughing.

"Good thing, too. The company was going under. I had to work all the hours that God made just to keep it going, get mom back in the land of the living, and put Bert through dental school. But it was the *least* I could do. He still can't snorkel properly."

The two woman giggled.

"Don't worry, I'll get my job back. Tony likes me."

There was a pause.

"Not like *that*! Well, maybe he does. But I don't. Anyway, they always need people, so after my exams I'll probably work full time again -- for the summer. It's a shit job, but it keeps me from sponging off the parents."

"Do you need money?" Lisa stirred her coffee and set the spoon down.

"I don't wanna do that, Lis."

"Neither do I, but I thought I'd *ask*."

"Call it a graduation present."

"Come *on*! I owe you like a million dollars *now*. I *can't*!"

"Of course you can! All you have to do is say yes and buy some decent luggage. Rome! Florence! Venice!"

"Oh, Lis."

"Here comes the steward; we'll ask *him*. See what he thinks."

"No! Lisa, **no**!"

Lisa straightened up in her chair.

"Madame," he said, setting down the brandy, "Mademoiselle."

"Monsieur, s'il vous plaît," Lisa spoke in rapid French, Lacey caught "Roma" and another word or two, but not much else. When she was finished, the steward answered and they both laughed.

"What did you tell him?"

"I said -- no, I'll tell you next year -- in Rome."

"Lis, I can't say yes. A lot of things can *happen* in a year. Who knows? Maybe you'll meet somebody."

"I doubt that."

"You know what I mean."

Lisa lifted her brandy with her palm and warmed it in her hand.

"Okay, I'll leave it alone. But let's do *this*: I'll send you a Christmas card with the itinerary. Bert's probably going to take the kids skiing in

Canada again this year, so when you get the card, call me. How's that?"

"Okay," Lacey said, feeling mean.

And it was the next day or maybe the next that they landed at Côte d'Azur.

It wasn't sadness; it was *worse* than that. It was the utter futility of normal. They had left each other at the airport. Lisa had a connecting flight, so there was no time for any real goodbyes -- just a few inane remarks, a long tired hug, and Lisa holding Lacey's hands together and pulling them to her lips.

"I had such a wonderful time," she said, smiling and warm, and kissed Lacey's fingers. The two women stood for a few seconds, wordless.

"Au revoir," Lisa said in a whisper and turned and walked away. Lacey watched her go, saw her change, almost immediately, from a casual strolling tourist to a clip-stepped deliberate professional. And then she simply melted away into the crowd. That was the *first* alone, standing on the edge of Europe, unable to step off -- the heavy Versace bag Lisa had bought her, keeping her from floating into the air. And the strange thing was she would have *willingly* floated away because the other alternative was -- *what now*? And she honestly hadn't thought about that. She hadn't ever considered that Lisa and Lacey would eventually end. So she just stood there.

"I should go home," she thought. But ... she didn't even know where to get her suitcase --

Shannon's suitcase. Shannon? A faraway friend that Lacey vaguely remembered.

"I should probably go home."

And she did go home, instinctively, moving through time and space until the taxi stopped somewhere familiar -- and her key fit the lock, and she closed the door behind her, exhaled and left her suitcase in the hall. She sat down in the living room, under the windows on the same brown sofa. She slid the Versace bag Lisa had bought her off her shoulder onto the floor and lay down. She hugged the throw pillow to her head with both hands, and after a few minutes she fell asleep.

Days, weeks, even months later, things hadn't changed. She'd got her job back at the coffee shop when she showed up in a too-tight t-shirt and offered Tony a bag of dead grandma guilt for firing her. She eventually went back to school, and even though her exams were difficult, they weren't *impossible*. Her GPA suffered, but she passed. After the *final* final, she met Shannon and a few others for drinks. Too much tequila and she started to cry.

"You must miss your grandma a lot," Shannon said. It didn't help, and Lacey went home. She called the parents. Talked to her brothers. Telephoned an ex-boyfriend, but that ended badly with her screening her phone calls and anxiously counting the days until her period. After that, she mostly just went to work and came home.

She felt tired, used up -- as if she'd been washed too many times and now she was gray and dull and shapeless -- like some discarded dishcloth tucked in the elbow of the pipes under the sink.

After resisting the urge for several weeks, she googled Lisa and *found* her, smiling and warm, at a Farmer's Market in Milwaukee. The website was Radisson River, a family-owned food processing company in Wisconsin, and Lisa was the majority owner and CEO. She was married with two children, and the company made a variety of condiments and sold them in Japan. And after that, Lacey didn't care anymore.

She tried texting but couldn't figure out what to say, so she just said "hi" a couple of times, but that didn't get a response. Finally, she telephoned and a very nice woman said Ms. Anderson was out of the office but she could leave a message and Ms. Anderson would return her call -- "Who could she say was calling, please?" It was all too confusing for Lacey. She didn't want to talk to Ms. Anderson; she wanted to talk to *Lisa*, and she couldn't say who was calling because she didn't know who she was supposed to be.

"What is this concerning?"

"That's fine. I'll call back, thank you."

But she *didn't* call back; it was too difficult. So she went to work and came home and usually watched TV most of the night. She ate mac and cheese and frozen pizza and leftovers from the coffee shop. She got angry with Lisa, angry with herself, and half cleaned the apartment several times. She went clubbing for awhile and found another ex-boyfriend, but that didn't last. She decided this was stupid and she needed to get on with her life -- but that didn't last either. And by the end of the summer, she'd fallen into sleeping late and doing nothing, unconsciously caught in the slow leak of her life, watching the endless tick of minutes accumulating -- until it was time to sleep again.

The telephone rang on Wednesday afternoon. It woke Lacey and before she was conscious enough to ignore it, she picked it up and said hello.

"Hi, Lace. This is Lisa." There was a giggle, "Remember me?"

Foggy with sleep and fooled by her dreams, Lacey sank her head back into the pillow, relieved.

"Oh, Lis. Where've you been? I was so worried."

There was a second of silence.

"Wisconsin?" Lisa questioned.

Lacey didn't understand and there was more silence.

"Are you alright, Lace? Did I call at a bad time?"

"Yeah -- uh. No, I'm good. No -- um -- I must have fallen asleep. I -- uh -- What time is it?"

"Lace. It's the middle of the afternoon."

Lace? *Nobody* called her Lace. *Lisa* called her Lace. Lisa? Lisa!

"Lisa?"

"Just so. Surprised?"

Lacey *was* surprised.

She sat up on the sofa, closed her eyes tight, yawned and stretched her free arm out in front of her, fingers wide.

"What are you *doing*? Where *are* you?"

"I'm at home, but I'm coming to see you -- tomorrow. I've got some people I need to meet and some papers I have to sign, so I'm going to fly in, in the morning. I'll be busy all day but we can have dinner at my hotel. Okay? Say, seven?"

Lacey had talked to Lisa so many times in the last few months: in the shower, on the bus, at work, slowly falling asleep. She had said so many things to her, but now all she could manage was:

"Yeah, that's good. Yeah. Seven."

"You remember the hotel?"

"Uh huh -- yeah, no problem."

"Okay, it'll be great. You can tell me all your good stories and we'll drink wine and have that chocolate -- uh -- chocolate, whatever we had last time. I'm at work, Lace. I have to go, but I'll see you tomorrow. Okay?"

"Yeah."

"Okay, go back to sleep. See you tomorrow. Bye."

"Bye, Lis." But the phone was already dead.

Lacey didn't remember what happened next -- it was so long ago. But the ache was real -- she could remember that -- and the excitement and the hurt at the very bottom of her belly and how all the anger dissolved away like sugar in the rain when she saw Lisa sitting in the restaurant. She tried to appear casual. She stopped and looked deliberately where Lisa *wasn't*, but Lisa was already out of her chair, the purpose of her heels sounding on the wooden floor. When Lacey turned her head back, Lisa was there and she had her hands on Lacey's shoulders. She pulled her in like a plush toy.

"Oh, I've missed you. I've missed you. I've *missed* you." Lisa said, running all the words together.

Lacey knew the voice and the feel, but it was the smell of Lisa's hair and her makeup that made Lacey cry. She swallowed as Lisa stepped back and ran her hands down Lacey's arms to hold her in place.

"You let your hair grow. I *love* it. Come," Lisa said, turning and pulling Lacey along, "I've got the same table we had last time."

The server was already there, holding the chair out for her. Lacey stopped and carefully touched the tears out of the corner of her eye and then sat down.

"I've ordered Côtes du Rhône something or other. Can you remember what we drank on the river? Are you hungry? No? Right, we'll look at the menus later. Let's try the wine and talk for a minute," Lisa said, sitting down, pushing the menus aside and pointing at Lacey's glass -- all in one motion. The server immediately poured wine for Lacey.

"Pick it up. Pick it *up*." Lisa reached across with her wine glass. There was a loud "cling" as the two women misjudged the distance between them and the glasses collided. A couple of people turned their heads to the sound.

"I'm so excited to see you." Lisa sipped her wine, "How *are* you? You sounded terrible over the phone. I thought I was going to have to come and pick up the pieces."
"I'm fine, Lis."
And Lacey knew she was going to Rome.

Time got lost in the big restaurant and they lingered and talked. They remembered Europe vividly -- retold and laughing. And when Lisa asked, Lacey told her about Tony and the tight t-shirt and sailing through her exams and how things were good and she was going to be an aunt for the fourth time (last brother.) Lisa had pictures of her children and Lacey asked questions in the right places. Ben was going to be a senior ("God, I feel old!") and Courtney was already picking out universities and working on the second love of her life. Work? Work was busy -- too busy ... but ... I've been doing that all day, let's not talk about it tonight. What about ...? And, so, by the time they were sharing dessert (poached pears/two forks) the evening was gone and the restaurant had filled up. It was clattery and loud, and both women were having trouble keeping the noise out of their conversation, so they decided to take their coffee on the 6th floor patio. The city lights were already on and they sat for a moment, admiring the night.
"It's beautiful up here."
"I've been staying at this hotel forever, and I've never done this before."
"How come?"

"Just never thought about it. I was always too busy -- uh -- doing other things."

The night was close, warm to the touch. The faint and full glare of the buildings around them hung in the air, searching their light into the night and hiding the two women together in intimate shadows. The sound of the city, low and breathing, was somewhere beyond them -- below them -- holding them up. There was a red goblet candle on the table, and they watched its tiny flame trembling between them and wondered what to say next.

"I found an apartment in Rome?" Lisa said tentatively.

"We need to talk, Lis."

"I know, but I don't know what ..." Lisa's voice trailed off.

"I need to know what we're *doing*."

"It's not very complicated. It doesn't have to be complicated. We had a great time, and I want to do it again."

"That's not what I mean. I need to know what we're doing? You and I?"

Lisa looked beyond Lacey into the night.

"You're spending all this money. I can't keep up with that. And *then* what? Are you going to disappear again? Am I just supposed to *wait*? God, I've been miserable for four months, wondering what was going on."

"I'm sorry, Lace. I thought you needed time to think. You said you did. Then when you called, I didn't know what to do."

"You knew I called?"

"Call display. Jennifer knew who you were before you hung up."

Lacey looked stricken. Lisa reached over, took Lacey's hand and pulled it across the table toward her. She covered it with her other hand and held it there.

"Look, Lace, *this is me*. I'm filthy rich, I've got a great job that's tons of hard work, but I wouldn't trade for anything. I've got two beautiful children who are a pain in the ass and I happen to like my husband -- just not that much. But the bottom line is I want something more than that. Something that's just for me. Unfortunately, when a woman in my position climbs above the glass ceiling, everybody thinks they have the right to look up her skirt. I just refused to give them the opportunity. I have a lot of people depending on me. So I take my private affairs outta town."

"Okay," Lacey interrupted, "But what am I? Where do I fit in? Why are you doing all this for a stranger?"

"We're not exactly strangers, Lace. We *slept* together."

"Yeah, in the same bed. But we didn't *do* anything. It's something I'd remember."

Lisa let go of Lacey's hand.

"Okay, but... This is what I want to do. We feel *right*, Lace. We have from the moment I met you. You're funny. You're happy. You're smart. You're kind. You're full of life. You understand me -- or at least you try to. You're all the things I've never been and everything I've ever wanted."

"I'm not gay." Lacey said, shaking her head.

The night was long and quiet and longer still.
"I'm *not*."
"Does it matter?"

Lacey looked at the questions in Lisa's eyes and didn't have any answers. But feeling the warm night holding her, watching the desperate little red fire shivering in front of her and seeing Lisa sitting across the table, smiling and warm, Lacey *did* feel alive, and, strangely, she felt *happy*. For the first time in months, she felt as if she were Lacey again -- and that she was everything Lisa said she was. She reached across and clasped Lisa's hand.

"I don't care, if *you* don't."

The next day felt different. It *was* different. There was something in the morning light that was -- was -- Lacey didn't know *what* it was She opened the curtains to find it. She made the bed. She washed dishes. Lisa called from the airport to say goodbye. "I have to run. Call me if you need me. I'll talk to you at Christmas." After that, Lacey found two big green garbage bags. She went through her apartment, filled them up with four months of pizza boxes, trash and her miserable summer. She dragged them thumping down the stairs and threw them out. She registered for school, went to the grocery store, bought real food, and for the first time in weeks, showed up for work on time. *That* was it -- *time*. Time. That was what was different. It sounded funny when Lacey said it out loud, and she wasn't really sure what it meant, but it was *real* -- like something touchable.

That year, Lacey went home for Thanksgiving and nearly got outnumbered by the parents, but, fortunately, the brothers showed up and turned them into Grandma and Grandpa. Rescued, Lacey relaxed and very soon she realized that "How's school?" "Are you cooking anything?" and "We worry about you." *weren't* accusations. They were just questions, and there was nothing wrong with being Lucinda Ann, responsible daughter -- or Aunt Lucy -- or Wayne, Frank and Jerry's little sister. In the end, they were all just Lacey, and being Lacey was kinda fun. She relinquished her room and slept on the basement sofa. She peeled potatoes, watched football, played video games and stayed away from the stove. She found some high school friends for drinks and listened to their stories, told a lie or two herself and flirted with somebody's husband. And she found herself *enjoying* herself -- remembering that real life was normal. Yet -- and with no regret -- she discovered this world was not *her* world anymore. Her home -- her *real* home -- was three flights up and looked into the street, and she lived her own life there.

She took another shift at the coffee shop for the extra money -- four evenings a week instead of three -- and spend the other nights studying hard, turning into a library rat the rest of the time. There it was again, *time*. It seemed to telescope -- expanding and contracting to fill the space all around Lacey. Sometimes, yesterday was several weeks ago and sometimes last month was yesterday. But in it all -- all the time available --

the *beginning* was France and the next stop was Italy.

Lacey didn't go to her parents' house at Christmas. She pleaded work and school and even a little illness and promised to come before New Year's. Instead, she waited for Lisa, hoping she'd come, thinking she would, planning for her visit. But Lisa *didn't* come. She sent a set of Versace luggage that arrived on Christmas Eve with a simple Hallmark card that read "Merry Christmas. See you in May. L." And she telephoned. And for over two hours on the night before Christmas, they were Lisa and Lacey, talking to each other in the dark, surrounded by the night. Then, in the last week of April -- which was two weeks later -- Lacey packed a suitcase and waited for Lisa.

And they went to Rome like two pilgrims looking for a private eternity. The apartment was small but it had a balcony, and if you leaned the right way, you could see St. Peter's -- so the next morning they walked it. It wasn't very far, but they stopped at every opportunity, and by the time they found the long wall of the Vatican, the tourist lines were too long to conquer. So they abandoned organized religion, found an alley full of trattoria and put their feet up. They ate bread and cheese and spicy sausage, drank a couple of thick glasses of wine, and after that they were never really tourists again.

It was easy to live in Rome. They called themselves sisters and said they were teachers. They drank coffee in the morning and red wine at night. They ate and laughed and told each other stories. They flirted with the men in the shops on their street. They walked and got lost and walked again, seeing most of the "sites" by accident. They discovered they liked churches, dark with Caravaggio, and weekends in the park loud with children. They danced behind Fendi sunglasses and watched the rain from their balcony. It was spring. They bought flowers. The two single beds were on opposite walls and they stayed that way. Sometimes, Lacey would see Lisa, look at her and wonder if this was the woman she wanted -- or was supposed -- to be. And without ever trying, Lisa showed Lacey the quiet confidence of *power* -- raw and deliberate.

"Never. It doesn't matter what Bert thinks; he's *not* going to divorce me. I've got a roomful of lawyers who play golf with Satan ... *and win*. He'd end up with a handful of dental floss -- and he *knows* it."

And sometimes Lacey saw Lisa looking at her. She'd seen that look before -- boy-shy and uncertain -- and that wasn't the Lisa that Lacey wanted to see.

They thought of taking the train to Venice, but never really did it. Although they *did* take a bus tour to Pompeii and had a picnic. They went to a flower show, saw a parade, watched fireworks, and late one night, crashed somebody's wedding and danced with the bride. But mostly it was easy to live in Rome, and then one day, unexpectedly, it was time to go home.

Lisa left Lacey at the airport and Lacey watched her go, shouting "*Arrivederci*!" into the crowd. She saw

Lisa's hand in the air, laughed, turned on her heels, and with abrupt purpose, went home.

That year, Lisa came to Lacey's graduation, sitting smiling, up front and incognito. They went for drinks after the parents went to bed. Lacey got a job with an investment company, but the hours were brutal and she had to dress for success. Six months later, she quit and went back to the coffee shop fulltime. Lisa called on Christmas Eve, and in May, they went to Spain.

That year, they really *were* pilgrims, walking the *Camino de Santiago* until, muscled, tanned and tired, they caught a train south. They bought bikinis in Malaga and spent the rest of the month drinking sangria and playing on the resort beaches of Costa del Sol. One night, far from sober, they got tiny matching "LOL" tattoos, just below the tan line. It was the year Tony got fired, and Lacey became assistant manager. It was the year the parents decided to sell the house. It was the year Ben went to Dental School.

"No, Lace. Bert *isn't* Ben's father. Haven't I told you that story before? Ben's father was a paper salesman from Chicago. I was a senior in high school, working weekends at the plant, and this guy -- you should've *seen* him, Lace! He was drop-dead *gorgeous*. He drove a silver Vette and he had a smile that was just pure panty remover. Anyway, he's selling paper -- uh -- I don't really remember the details. But he took me to lunch and then he took me to dinner and he was from Chicago and ... *Don't give me that look*. He didn't know I was 17, and he definitely didn't know I was the owner's daughter. Besides, I kinda *launched* myself at him. The poor guy really didn't have a chance. Anyway, a couple of months later, all hell broke loose. Trust me, Lace, you don't want to be rich-bitch pregnant in a small town. It's *amazing* how many faces your friends have. So my parents and Bert's parents got together, and we were married that summer."

"What about Ben? Does he *know*?"

"Well, since Bert and I are the only ones left who actually *know* the truth, we decided to just leave it alone. Sometimes the truth isn't the best way to go."

The next year they went to Amsterdam, or was it London? London -- *then* Amsterdam? Amsterdam, then London? Lacey couldn't remember without thinking hard. But somehow that's what happened; somewhere, without Lacey realizing it, the years just starting clicking away. Ben finished school and went to work with his father. The parents *did* sell the house and moved into that stupid condo nobody liked. Jerry and Jennifer had another baby. Wayne and Madison split up, got back together and finally divorced for good. Courtney got accepted at UCLA, moved to California and Lisa cried on the telephone. And somewhere, after Amsterdam (or was it London?) unable to control herself, Lacey found a lesbian lover -- in fact, *more* than one. In fact, now that Lacey thought about it, quite a *few* more than one. It wasn't that she felt the need especially, or even *cared,* but it just seemed like the right thing to do.

But that was the problem. Plagued with good intentions, Lacey had decided to do the right thing and everything had gone to hell from there. Actually, that wasn't strictly true. She hadn't *planned* any of it. She'd kinda fallen into it, like Alice down the rabbit hole. But that wasn't true either -- not really. Alice had never been to Wonderland before, and Lacey'd been going there for nearly ten years. She was an accomplice, not just a participant, and in the cold, dark soul of 4 o'clock in the afternoon, she *knew* that. Sitting on the brown sofa, looking out the window on a chilly all alone Christmas Eve, she knew, despite the stories she'd been telling herself, she was just as responsible for Lisa and Lacey as Lisa was. After all these years of living two different lives, juggling half-truths and lies, keeping her time with Lisa safely on the other side of the Atlantic, Lacey understood that. There was no longer any distance between the two women, and there was no use dressing it up in good intentions. She remembered way back when, on the boat -- the *first* boat -- down the Rhone, she'd asked:

"You're so complicated. There's all these layers. But I still don't know what kind of a person gives all this to someone they hardly know?"

Lisa didn't hesitate: "The same kind who accepts it."

She should have known then. She *did* know then. The truth was, she just didn't want to admit it. She didn't want to think too hard about what makes a person put their real life on hold to play house once a year. Lisa understood and was willing, but Lacey had spent years diligently avoiding even thinking about it. It had been so simple. She had been so happy. So... But now -- now was *different*, even though Lisa had called, several times, and every time had managed to reassure Lacey that everything was fine and that things were alright -- now was Christmas Eve. Christmas Eve and without Lisa, Lacey realized she was no longer a girl, and she was sitting alone with a bottle of Côtes du Rhône -- and she had never intended to end up this way.

The irony was Lacey never intended to do anything -- not that night -- not ever. It was just the night. The warm spring night and the light -- the half light smoothing through the glass wall open cabin door, fluttering the winter-length lace curtains. And the distant sounds of music, low over the water, elegant and primitive, and the Danube slowly dreaming them along. They were like shadows in the floating false twilight, unreal phantoms of themselves. Lisa on her stomach, half asleep and half covered in folded white marble. Lacey sitting in the doorway, all legs and carefully balanced. They'd been talking and drifting and talking and now quiet again, time out of mind.

"God, I'm tired," Lisa sighed without actually speaking. "We must have walked a hundred miles today."

Hypnotized by the shape of Lisa, statue grey in the teasing light, Lacey heard all the words but they were just sounds, female noises exhaled into the darkness. It was the deep even whisper of Lisa's breath Lacey had been listening to, the slender tremors that moved her shoulders, slight and rising like a long lingering pulse. Unconsciously, Lacey had fallen into their rhythm -- breathing in and breathing out. And she could see her there -- Lisa -- her face, her arm tucked under her chin, the fall of her hair, the sloping muscles of her back, the swell of her hips, all sculpted out of a moment in time. Time that was going to vanish, telescope into a memory and maybe even disappear. There was a deep sadness in that, that Lacey didn't want to understand. She wanted *forever*. She wanted it for her -- she wanted it for always -- but more than anything else, she knew she wanted it for Lisa.

Lacey pushed herself out of the doorway, took three deliberate steps and knelt at the side of the bed. She put her hand on Lisa's back. She could feel the warm of the touch between them. She moved her hand down across the tiny soft hair in the small of Lisa's back. She could feel Lisa moving to follow her hand. She leaned forward and softly blew a long point of air up Lisa's spine. Lisa twisted her shoulders, pushing her hips down into the bed. Lacey moved her face forward and kissed the intimate hollow between Lisa's shoulders, wetting her lips with her tongue. There was a sound from Lisa's throat, deep and moist. Lacey brushed Lisa's hair away. She could see Lisa's eyes, half awake and half aware. She ran her tongue slowly across Lisa's shoulder bone and kissed her on the neck. She could feel the pulse jump. She kissed her again. She reached under Lisa's cheek, turned her face and held it in her hands and then she kissed her, opening her lips with her tongue. It was luscious, long and tender with desire. She could feel Lisa's hand reaching into her hair. Lacey moved her lips across Lisa's cheek and, ragged with breath, kissed her again -- bigger, fuller, more demanding. She could feel Lisa's body reaching up to meet her. Lacey moved her mouth back and holding Lisa in her hands, paused -- waited. Lisa opened her eyes and the two women looked at each other. There were no words. Lacey leaned forward.

"We can't do this." Lisa said, turning her head.

Lacey stopped.

"We can't, Lace." Lisa pleaded, "We just can't."

Lacey smiled. "Yes, we can," she said, slyly. "I've been practicing."

Lisa turned her hips and tried to put her feet on the floor, but the sheets held onto her and she kicked her legs. Lacey leaned forward again and Lisa grabbed her wrist.

"No, Lace." she said firmly, trying to sit up.

Lacey stayed on her knees, dumb with confusion. Unable to kick free from the sheets, Lisa pushed Lacey from the wrist and, off balance, Lacey sat down heavily. Lisa let go and, in one motion, swung her legs over the side of the bed and stood up. She stepped over Lacey's knee and her leg brushed against Lacey's arm.

"Don't!" Lisa said, finally and completely, stepped around the corner into the bathroom and slammed the door.

Hours later, or maybe ten minutes, Lisa opened the door and turned on the light. Lacey was back in the doorway, numb in the breeze. Lisa just stood there, in the green and gold #12 shapeless sports shirt she always slept in. More time passed.

"Say something," Lacey said, without looking.

"It was you who said no. Way back when: 'I'm not gay. Don't expect me to be.' You *said* it."

"I know I did, but ... I thought ... I just thought."

"What did you think?" Lisa cut her off, "Rub the old girl the right way and that'll keep her happy?"

"No, Lis. It isn't like that. You don't understand."

"No, Lacey. You're the one who doesn't understand. You made the rules. You made *all* the rules. Have they changed now? Nobody told me. I didn't get that memo."

"I just thought..."

"No, you didn't. You didn't think about tomorrow. Or the next day. You didn't think about where this little escapade was going to leave *me*. You're not gay, Lacey. Did you think I wasn't going to notice?"

There were so many things to say, so much Lacey had to explain. But Lisa cut her off again.

"I know it was never me." She said matter-of-factly. "It isn't me you want. I can live with that. I *have* lived with that. But why is it always about you -- always?"

"Me?" Lacey scolded, before she thought, "Me? You're the one who's going to leave me standing at the airport. And what do I get after that? A couple of phone calls. Three -- if I'm lucky. And maybe, when you can fit me into your schedule, you show up for a visit. But, believe me, I don't hold my breath waiting anymore. And do we ever do anything? No! We pretend we do, but we don't. And I can't come and see you. God, no! Your precious reputation couldn't take *that*. I don't even know those people and I'm scared of them. Bullshit! It's not always about me."

"You do the same thing."

"Did you just *hear* yourself? You're pathetic. If you want to stay in the closet, fine, but you're keeping me in there with you. And it's not even my closet."

"That's not true."

There was a long pause.

"We've been doing this for eight years, Lis. Eight *years*. And in all that time, you've never been to my apartment. Never. Not once. It's a ten minute cab ride from your hotel. I should know; I've done it often enough. You're so damn worried about where this leaves you. Where does that little fact leave *me*? Where has it ever left me? I was just trying to be nice. I wanted to be nice to you. It's all I ever wanted to do."

There was silence -- a long silence.

"Turn off the light and go to bed, Lis. I'm too tired to fight with you, anymore."

The next day was long and sunny and sad -- and slowly they apologized to each other. It cut both ways and the hurt wouldn't go away. Despite their best intentions, the distance between them was too uncomfortable to maintain. Intimate strangers unable to look at each other. That evening, they decided that the next day, in Vienna, they would cut things short and just go home. And that's what they did.

At the airport, Lacey hurried Lisa along and Lisa lingered. Finally, they both ran for Lisa's plane, and it was a quick hug -- the first touch -- and then goodbye. Lisa called as soon as she got home and many times after that. Each time, there was more Lisa and less distance.

Lacey stayed home that year. The parents' condo was too small, the brothers weren't interested and honestly neither was she. She took night courses in accounting and decided to learn French. There was time for such things.

And now it was the afternoon before Christmas and Lacey was pouring more wine into her glass when the telephone rang. She spilled some, grabbing the phone.

"Hi, Lace. This is Lisa. Merry Christmas."

"Merry Christmas, Lis."

There was a pause.

"Do you remember the first cruise we took, Lace, down the Rhone?"

"Sure."

"Remember the night I embarrassed you talking to the steward?"

"Yeah, I remember. You never did tell me what you said to him."

"That's what I need to tell you now. I told him that we weren't a mother and daughter. I told him that we hardly knew each other and that I was an old dyke trying to seduce you into my bed. And you know what he said to me? He said, 'Don't worry, Madame. You're not fooling anyone. The only one who doesn't know it is your girlfriend.' I'd like to go back to Paris and start over, Lace. Do you want to come?"

------/\------

....The Bookstore on Elliott Street

There was a bookstore on Elliott Street. It was half as wide as it was long, with three slender aisles and books on shelves stacked higher than a woman could reach. It had a big window and a wooden glass door that was brown, and the paint was peeling until he repainted it. It had stairs in the back that went up to an apartment that sat on the tops of the trees and overlooked the street. He knew it was there. He hadn't dreamt it. So why couldn't he find it?

For a few moments he stood stupid in the sun, shielding his eyes in the brilliance. His memories were different. They were rainswept and cold: the pavement headlight shiny and slick with traffic lights; the buildings granite and bitter moss green; the trees bony and small, their tough little fingers digging into the sky. And the low clouds were angry grey, with an early darkness so heavy they bowed the heads of the people walking underneath them. It was always deep into autumn on Elliott Street and always late in the afternoon.

Just in case, he checked the street name.

He crossed the street and walked along, watching the other side, trying to remember who was what where.

"The bakery; something; something; the laundry (you had to walk downstairs) s-s-something; the chicken place (it was Greek.) The bank -- no, that was on this side, on the corner."

He stopped to look for the bank, but it had disappeared. In front of him, halfway down the block, was a restaurant with tables and chairs out in the sunshine, on the sidewalk. He walked up and sat down.

"The bakery; the chicken place -- Adonis? Adidas? Athena? The grocery store, with vegetables." He made a sliding gesture with the flat of his hand, to show the shape of the outside bins to his memory.

"The bus stop; the theater. No, that's too far. That's the next street." He started again.

"You have to get it yourself."

He stopped pointing in his mind and turned toward the voice.

"I beg your pardon?"

"You have to go get it yourself. There's no server."

He looked at her, like a moron.

"At the counter. No server."

"Oh," he said, "Thank you."

He got up to go inside and had to pause to locate the door.

"Are you lost or something?"

"No. Actually, I was just trying to remember something."

The place wasn't a restaurant at all, but a coffee bar, part of a chain. The tables were round and the chairs quite obviously didn't match. There were crates in the corner marked with big black stamps and the shelves were loaded with tidy odds and ends from the coffee trade. Everything was meticulously arranged to look gathered and haphazard. Country casual – he knew the style. It felt sterilized. The boy behind the counter was noticeably pleased to see him, so he bought a medley of robust flavors at an exorbitant price, and, despite the difficulty, finally managed to find the cream and sugar and honey and cinnamon. etc, etc, etc.

He went back outside to the place he'd been sitting, and smiled at the girl who had spoken and she smiled back at him. He looked across the street, but now he was tired of trying his memory, so he just slouched in the sun.

The summer had been lazy at the bookstore. She had worn thin, printed dresses that touched her and danced when she walked, so, in the mornings, he'd go outside and sweep the sidewalk and wash the windows and finally he re-painted the door and all the trim. But by noon, the day would settle on them; the sun, striped through the blinds in narrow, dusty bars; the overhead lights shallow in the brilliant, shadowed afternoon. The air, too heavy to move, just floated, baking the color out of the book covers and drying out the glue. So they would sit, like hot zombies, hidden from the sun at the low table behind the counter, and, for hours, among the food wrapper or pizza boxes or chicken bones, they would suck on sticky, melting drinks and play backgammon. Once she tried to teach him how to smoke, and once she cut his hair and once she fell asleep in her chair so he sat and chatted with Jay Gatsby in the drowsy hours and prayed that nobody would bother them.

    But the bookstore wasn't a place for pretty weather. It was a place with chilly edges. A place where the lights were meager and not quite warm enough for the coming night. It was a place of cold feet and thick socks. A place where the rain blew hard against the windows and teakettles steamed long before they ever boiled.

    Instinctively, he reached for his coffee and drank at it, holding it close to his face. He had long since learned how to smoke and now he was almost always trying to quit, but he lit one anyway and blew a lungful straight into the sky, half expecting it to billow out into a mushroom against the ceiling. He looked at the girl who had spoken to him. She was bent over the plastic table, carefully reading her book. He imagined he could almost see her lips move. He wondered what she was reading. Something frothy perhaps, with broad characters and a shallow plot. She had shiny hair and a reasonable oval face with cute features that were so standard they were almost familiar. She had an even, trim body with strong legs that she kept tucked under her chair, and her arms were bare.

"Protein and tennis" he thought. "Too old to be a student. Probably a teacher -- brand-new, and the smartest person she knows. The pillowcases on her bed match the sheets, but only her teddy bears know that for sure. A professional virgin, she probably writes sugary verse on colored paper and makes little circles when she dots her i's. And her name is... Caitlin."

He set the cup down, satisfied with himself. It was too hot for coffee, anyway.

He went back to the street he remembered, following his long-forgotten steps coming from school, past all the shops. He remembered hurrying along the sidewalk, every moment precious, only half-acknowledging people he'd known for as long as his life. A veteran youth, they were already part of his past. For she had changed him by then, directing his hands, softening his touch, slowly willing him to her purpose. So that he had no time to waste on a drycleaner's smile, or Jack and Brian, or the causes of the Industrial Revolution. Everything that wasn't in her presence was a stumbling dream. She was a holy secret that smeared his eyes for the rest of the world. And then he would be there, the small bell over the door tripping his vision on again. She would pour them tea and they would talk in low tones together, cuddled by the marbled autumn clouds that slowly sank them in darkness. Their faces slipping away, their bodies blending into the shadows, becoming only movement. Simply being near each other again worked like a steeping anesthetic, and, sheltered in the thick rows of books, they would disappear together and, invisible, watch the street happen past them -- like a dim film in a dark theater. Then, like a magician, she would turn on the lights and the street would vanish, and they could be alive again; the window just a large, dark mirror that sealed them into their own reflections.

Then they could breathe again, insistently going about the business of a bookstore, like actors in a domestic scene. They would find tasks or invent them and happily call to each other across the shop with trivial inquires and unneeded information, slowly manipulating themselves closer together as it became time to shut the shop. Then, when it was just past time, he would ask and turn the sign to CLOSED and lock the door, while she gathered the money and turned out the lights. They would carefully make their way to the back of the shop in the darkness, and there, surrounded and held by the towers of books, he would touch her, for the first time.

He could sense where she was and feel her warmth through her clothes and he would hold her against the books and she would form to his body, pulling him into her. Sometimes the stairs were too far away and the beginning of night too close, and they would slip down the black spines, awkwardly fumbling in the dark. And she would touch his face, holding his breath in her fingers. On the floor, she would move, twisting her clothes urgently kicking at the books on the bottom shelf to make room. He would hold her head up in his hands, cradling it to his shoulder, the muscles in his back tight. And she would cling to him, the palms of her hands firm at his waist. And they would lose themselves in the dark, pulling it closer around them, like a cloak, their fingers gripping the edges, until they were wrapped together, there, at the bottom of the darkness.

"Hell-o, hell-o. Sorry I'm late. Have you been waiting long?"

A happy female voice tore tatters through his remembrances, without the slightest hesitation.

"Oh, Christ! Caitlin has a friend."

He straightened up in his chair, wiggling the tightness out of his fingers, and reached for his coffee, which was nearly cold. He looked at the woman-girl as she sat down. She was turned slightly away from him, but he could see a vague resemblance to Caitlin.

"Another protein ad," he thought. "They must stamp them out of a mold."

Their animated chatter irritated him. He wanted them to leave, to go shopping, or do lunch, or plan their success or something -- just leave him alone. He looked back across the street.

"If I could just remember," he said to himself. "It was right in here, somewhere."

But he couldn't, or wouldn't or the sun was too hot or the sky was too bright or those two over there were chirping and chatting or...

"It could be anywhere," he thought finally, realizing, for the first time, that he didn't really remember it at all, except from the inside. In fact... in fact... Damn! Up until now, it hadn't mattered, because, for so many years, all he'd needed was the *feel* of it. Everything else had been lost, melted away by the sweet gush of sadness that always spread through him, whenever he thought about it. Of course, at first, there'd been details -- details so tender he'd hardly touched them, so painful they made him dizzy. Was it guilt or anger that drove him out onto Elliott Street or just her calm, final voice that told him to go? And then everything was lost, all the colors bleeding away. The eyes of a springtime trapped in the shadows, caught in an aching memory of nothing gone wrong and too young to be so alone. And he shut his eyes tight, wincing at the remembered pain.

"And tell Matthew no cream," the high-toned voice called.

Caitlin stood hovering and then turned for the door of the coffee shop.

He lit another cigarette and watched her move as she walked away. He picked up the last of his cold coffee, swirled it in the cup and set it down.

"No, it's time to go," he thought, suddenly tired of it all. He looked back across the street and blew a long gush of blue smoke into the air. Out of the corner of his eye, he saw what was probably Caitlin's best friend – uh – probably – uh -- Ashley -- looking at him. He turned his head, and she glanced away, studying the traffic. She had a cute, familiar presence that only new women of her generation could manage.

It had been a bad idea, really. What was he hoping to accomplish -- coffee and cookies upstairs at the kitchen table? An afternoon, looking out the window? Twenty years of interesting stories? No, just the real feel of it all again, something to recharge his memory and give it color and endurance. Something to touch, even if it was only the walls.

The shop door banged shut as Caitlin returned with her hands full of coffee and sat down with her friend. He dropped his cigarette, stepped on it and pushed his chair back. It made a noise and both women looked at him. He tried to look back at them as he stood up, but the sunlight caught his eyes and made them squint. For a few full seconds, he stood, blinded, and then, without thinking, he stepped over to where they were sitting.

"Excuse me," he said, "Maybe you can help me?"

They both turned and looked up at him.

"Yes?" Caitlin asked

"Well, it sounds a bit crazy, but there used to be a bookstore across the street. It was just a little place, right in-uh-about the middle," he was speaking quickly. "I-uh-I used to go there when...well...you're probably too young...but maybe your – you - you've heard of it. It was quite popular way back when. Anyway, I...I can't seem to find it."

They looked back at him strangely – skeptical.

"Actually, are you from around here? I just assumed." He had been talking with his hands and turned them, palms up, and shrugged his shoulders at them.

"I just can't seem to find it."

"What was it called?"

He stood there all afternoon alone in the sun. He remembered the door and the brown paint that peeled off his fingers like another skin. The shine on the windows after he'd washed them. The long crack in the sidewalk that always filled with dirt, when he swept. The line of rust on the broken strut in the awning. The light that collected out of the evening into her eyes. The sweet taste of the way she smelled close to him, the ends of her fingers, the line of her throat, the feel of her face in his hands. And then he sagged forward under the entire weight of it.

"I don't know," he said quietly.

The two women continued to stare up at him.

"I did know – I – I don't know – I," he exhaled deeply, "I – I just don't remember."

"There is no bookstore on Elliott Street," Caitlin said finally.

He collected himself.

"I'm sure it was before your time. I'm sorry to bother you."

"No bother." And they turned their faces away, waiting for him to leave before they started their conversation again.

And he did leave, his long afternoon shadow gliding seamlessly in front of him, taking him back to his hotel. His large clean American-style hotel, that had no memory, no shadows, no real light, where everything was brisk and crisp and shiny. He went to the bar and found his people scattered around low tables, talking about positioning and the afternoon seminar he'd missed: "ADD the Advantage of Advertising". So he joined them. He liked his people and enjoyed the time they spent at these conventions, but somewhere he lost the trails of their conversations and somewhere he slipped quietly back to the sunshine on Elliott Street. And it may have been Margo Palmer from Research, hopelessly in love with Stephen Varneer and trying to flirt him into an affair, or maybe it was just the whiskey, but there in the lean-forward intimate scene of the air-conditioned night, he decided to go back. Go back and find whatever was left after a couple of decades of loss.

It didn't seem like such a good idea the next day -- it never does -- but right after breakfast he slipped out anyway, knowing he would be missed and knowing it would take some explaining. But his shadow easily slid him forward into the open sun and along the few streets to the coffee bar that was open, and so he ordered another blend of robust flavors from the same happy young man and then he sat down at the same table and...and...and. For nearly an hour he didn't even know where to start.

A deep shade crawled along the sidewalk and spoke to him.

"Jonny?"

Her hair was full, but not past her shoulders, with just the smallest touch of rust in the sun. She wore a bright striped t-shirt under an open blouse and jeans, everything just tight enough to suggest vanity.

"And," he thought, "with good reason."

"Jonny?" the shadow said again.

It had no face but it spoke to him. Fine known tones like breaths of music that had always played only in his head.

"They said it was you."

But it wasn't him. His name wasn't Jonny. It was Jonathan -- Mr. Hargraves. There'd been a mistake.

"Who are they?" he answered dumbly.

"My girls. They saw you here yesterday. And Matthew" she gestured, "called me when you came back. What are you doing?"

"I don't know. I was looking for you. The – the bookstore?"

He couldn't help it, two long tears overflowed the squinting corner of his eye, and he took the palm of his hand to smear them away.

"What happened to the bookstore?"

"The bookstore isn't here, Jonny. It was on Allen Road, one over. What are you doing? Are you alright?"

He wasn't sure. Maybe not? Maybe the somewhere dream wasn't and the only things waiting for him here were stones, black phantoms hard in the sunshine.

"May I sit down?"

And she did, and he could see her clearly. Her face was bright and happy like the first notes of a familiar song and all the ghosts of panic flared and vanished without leaving even a cinder in their passing.

"It's good to see you," she said and reached over to touch his hand.

There's a slender place between awareness and dreaming. We go there as children to daydream and play, and sometimes we find it again on the uneven edges of chancy sleep: tricks of thought suspended between our realities. He had spent the entire day there. Remembered now without tastes or shapes, just spaces, gaps that became beginnings with no ending marks. She was she, all of the parts and expectations completed. But now, sitting on the bathroom counter, blowing hard winds of smoke into the buzzing ceiling vent, he wanted to see it all again. Retrace his steps until something had size or weight – firmness. He arced a long ash into the toilet. The stark spa light of the bathroom was brilliant bright but cold, and there were the heavy sleeping sounds of Margo in the bed, snoring. And he was something less than he'd been yesterday or the day before, except he had one more memory – a shiny morning in the sun. He was tired, sleepy and weary, but he'd never gotten used to actually sleeping with someone else in his bed and it would be a nasty trick to wake Margo and send her back to her own room. So he sat, uncompleted, alone in the porcelain night.

The bookstore was gone. She'd given it up and rented the space but she still lived upstairs. It was a cooking shop now, with molded electric things that moved and mixed, new things with clever colours, things that had no smell. He had walked there with her at the end. But before that: she worked part-time for the library, her children were fun, laughing and light-hearted. They had diminutive names. Matthew, the boy at the counter, had been around for ages. When you have two daughters, it's surprising how many young men you get to meet. They were all at the university together, and no, she'd never married. He didn't remember Gary or Mrs. Higgins or that little fat man or the Sandersons, he died. But that was okay and where did he live? So far away! He told her he sold plastic pipe and she laughed. "I don't see it, Jonny." She said. But she asked him if he liked it and he said he did and she seemed pleased with that. And sitting in the sun for a couple of hours, they were he and she -- not Diane and Jonathan. And then it was time to go, and he went with her to the door, and she hugged him and kissed him on the cheek and said good-bye, and it was nice to see him.

    He pushed his cigarette like a dart into the air. It hit the toilet, foosted and died. The bathroom tiles were bright white with flecks of colours, so they were easy to keep clean. The stone at the door of the bookshop had been dim grey and there was a dull shine intercom in the wall. Like a failing addict, he had come back to it twice in the fading light evening before actually pushing the button.

"Yes?" it was a wrong mechanical sound.

"It's Jonathan. I – uh – I need to talk to you."

"Who? Jonny? – crackaly-crackle – What do you want?"

"I need to... Can I come up?"

There was a full pause.

"I'll – crackle crack – come down."

And then there was silence, and he stood waiting with his face leaning into the stone. She came through the door next to the kitchen shop and stood half behind it.

"What?" she said, and it was final.

He didn't know. Standing on the edge of the wilderness, it was vast and he was alone. So he just said.

"Do you actually know who I am?"

She slumped her forehead down against the door, annoyed. Then she looked up.

"No," she shook her head. "Not really. I do remember you. I do. But...sorry... it's been so many years. I just can't place you anywhere. I thought I did – uh – thought I could but..."

"How did your daughters know me?" He moved away from the door and stood a step into the street between the parked cars.

"You're in some old photographs. They've seen them a million times, and you haven't changed that much. Then, when you asked about the bookstore, they thought you might be somebody but they weren't sure." She smiled, "Last night, we got out the old albums and there you were. So, today, when Matthew called, I thought maybe I'd – I don't know – recognize you – remember something." She shrugged, "So I came round."

He stared at her.

"You looked so awful, so -- lost -- I just couldn't -- didn't have the heart."

"There's a frailty that comes with being a victim," he thought, "like old, folded paper finally crumbling away at the creases." And there was a shutter of hurt that came with that.

He lit another cigarette and placed the lighter carefully on the package, next to the disconnected smoke alarm. He looked at his watch roughly calculating the time.

"Three hours?" He thought, "Probably four."

That was too long. He couldn't hide in the toilet all night. Maybe he could?

"That's a terrible thing to do," he said, "You made it out like you knew – like you knew me. Like – like we…." He waved his hand between them.

"I'm sorry. I was trying to be nice. It was so long ago," she shrugged. "I didn't think..."

"But, you knew my name?"

She looked pained. This was getting difficult for her.

"It was written on the back of one of the pictures." she said, surrendered with guilt.

He stood between the cars, not trusting himself to step forward in case he staggered or fell.

"So, you don't remember anything?"

She half frowned her confession. It was brutally off-handed and his stomach flinched against it.

"What was I doing in the pictures?"

She gestured a question.

"What was I doing? I had to be doing something. What was I doing?"

"What are you talking about? I don't know. Several things. Standing there."

"What were you doing? Where were you?"

"What?"

"Alright then, how old is your daughter? The oldest one? How old is she?"

"I beg your pardon!"

"It's an easy question. How old is she? When was she born?"

"That's none of your business." She answered him angrily, straightening up from the door. "Who do you think you are, anyway?"

"It's who you think I am. That's the question."

That just sounded stupid. He bent his neck and looked up into the ceiling vent, stretching his legs forward and pointing his toes. When he looked down there was a small white hole in his left black sock. It didn't even look odd. He let his legs fall and adjusted the hotel bathrobe around him.

"There's something wrong with you," she said stepping forward and there was menace in it. She pointed two fingers at him. "You go away."

The door was slowly closing behind her.

"I don't know what you're doing, but I think it's time for you to go back to wherever you came from."

"You don't understand. I need to…"

"I don't care what you need," she cut him off.

"But…." he waved his hand again.

"I - was - just - trying - to - be - nice." Her fingers jabbed each word into him. "Now you go away."

She turned and just caught the door before it completely closed.

That was it. She was gone. But that was it – he realized it -- the voice. The same voice. The last voice. The one that had long years ago faded away from him. The rest had been false, a fake, a shiny morning that had tricked him. But the voice. That was real. There was no mistake. He could see it, see the sound of her in it. He stood up, dropped his cigarette in the toilet and pulled the handle.

There was a bookstore on Elliott Street. It wasn't some nocturnal schoolboy fantasy. He turned off the light, and in the solid black darkness, he could feel her there next to him, surrounded by all the stories the books could ever tell. He was tired. He pulled the warm robe around him and tightened his belly as if it hurt. He opened the door and felt just a little sad that he would have to wake Margo and tell her to go home.

------/\------

....Final Vinyl Cafe

It was nearly morning when the light woke her. It was a strange light that fanned out across the ceiling. Then she heard the articulate thump of car doors. She was awake then; fully awake, so she could distinguish steps in the gravel. Two sets -- one heavy, one light.. The big light from the motel courtyard shadowed through the room. She felt their presence, noiseless black and white, and she heard them, at the door. Closing it, locking themselves in. The erotic sounds of scuffling in the dark. Right next door, beside her, some few inches from her face. She listened, heart still in the darkness, willing her body motionless to hear. There was nothing for a long time; then the full fine groan of the bed. She relaxed and sat up slowly. She felt her feet touch and settle on the carpet. She sat still for a moment, not to wake him. His breathing was heavy and even.

She reached into the darkness and found the bulk knit of her sweater. She handled it quickly, found the neckline, and pushed her head through.

She stood up and stretched her arms into the sleeves and settled it down over her hips. It covered the top of her legs and held her against the chill of the night. She walked through the silver window light and sat opposite, facing the bed and the wall next door. She stretched her feet into the slanted light as if it were warm. It caught the sheen of new nail polish and glowed spots in the dark. The big knot knit hem of her sweater dug into the back of her legs. She lit a cigarette, cupping the instant flame, so as not to wake him. He hated smoking but she did it anyway.

"He's warm," she thought. "He has a sense of good and he's nearly always there -- comfortable – like the way we've arranged the furniture. She flipped a cigarette ash into the ashtray on the table and thought about their house. It was bright and green and alive with sunshine, neatly placed and open to the world. She looked back at the lump in the bed. She liked him and wished him well.

They had stumbled on this time together. A couple of stray vacation days, and even though the season was long over, they had decided to drive up. It wasn't winter yet but deep enough into the autumn that even the afternoons were chilly. They had tried walking, but the lake was windy off the water and the higher trails wet and muddy. They had bravely struggled around the first day but finally gave it up and settled in for thick grocery store novels and watery coffee. They no longer delighted in the discomfort of adventure. Sometimes they talked, but sometimes they didn't. They went to dinner and drank one or two too many and laughed at the old stories. Now there was one more day and then they would drive home, back over the same road again.

"I didn't water the fern," she thought.

The female noises from the next room were quicker now; high and slender, young and still slightly shrill, rising over the deep creaking that rhythmed against the wall. She felt embarrassed listening to the dark and embarrassed for the moist feeling. She carefully put the cigarette out and reached for her jeans. She wondered if they had heard her, that afternoon, just as urgent, straining, while he had labored over her, eyes clinched, stubbing against her, just slightly faster than the excitement could rise in her. Then all the noises combined when it was over more than finished, and they had covered and mewed until he dozed.

"Probably not," she thought.

She pulled on her jeans and found her purse and her tennis shoes. They were still damp from walking; she pulled the laces tight and tied them. Her feet were cold. She stopped and listened to him sleep. Then she opened the motel door and left, carefully closing the door on the final stretching female sounds and his deep steady breathing.

It was surprisingly dark outside where the light wasn't confined. And it was cold. She thought about going back for her jacket, but he would certainly hear her then and she didn't want to talk or answer questions or wait. So she didn't. She just drove away – out onto the highway until the motel lights vanished behind her and the brighter, cheaper café lights raced up to meet her – maybe a mile, maybe not that far. It looked closed, and even though she knew it wasn't, the thought made her realize how cold she was and how foggy the windows were and how silly it was to drive that fast.

She pulled onto the gravel and parked straight in front of the windows. The lot was nearly full of trucks and machines, great metal things with yellow claws and bent arms. They were cold lost, without human hands to move them, their windows black, their oils thick and their voices silent. They stood open and sat on their trucks, and took up space. She felt little standing by his car. There were small lights that shadowed her weakly against the building, barely holding out against the vast darkness. She went in and sat by the door.

The place was old, and bright, with chrome stools down a curved counter, and tables along the back wall by the high hole that looked into the kitchen. That was where the men were sitting. They were the men from the machines outside. Men with large coats and high laced boots. They stopped talking when she came in and some turned around to look at her. These men wore mitts and hats and worked in the weather, conjuring life into cold equipment. Now they sat close, grouped together, only a few heads showing over the broad backs that faced her.

The waitress automatically came with coffee. She was somebody's high school daughter with bright young eyes and a button green sweater that was unraveling at the cuff. She smiled and took back the menu. Her name was Laurie; her felt pen name tag said so. Laurie gave the rest of the pot of coffee to the men. The heat from their cups rose up over their heads and made them look like big barn animals, huddled and steaming in their stalls and blankets. She lit a cigarette and cupped her hands over the coffee. It was cold by the door.

The men talked in low tones, conscious of her. She shivered to herself against the faded brown vinyl of the booth. She swirled the end of her cigarette in the ashtray and tried to drink her coffee too fast, but it was hot and refused. She watched out the window, not comfortable enough to wipe the steam off so she could see clearly. And she smoked -- first with her left hand, then with her right. The men made it all a bad idea. They hadn't occurred to her. And now she was cold and it was dark, and she didn't have a jacket, and she was alone, and they felt so big and rutted, and she knew they knew she was there.

"Lady, uh, lady."

It was a test of wills. She wasn't scared. She knew that if she looked up she would drive them back to their hang-head huddle. She became exaggerated, like an actress, smoothing the ends of her hair, stiff fingering the ashes off her cigarette, pausing the coffee cup in front of her lips. She wished she wasn't so cold, just in case she shivered. She pulled her feet protectively back and underneath her; she didn't want them to see her dirty tennis shoes. Laurie's shape appeared, reflected in the window. She wondered if she was a party to this and they'd all laugh together when they'd driven her out. She hoped Laurie's laugh would be nervous. She turned directly at the young waitress.

"They..."

"Yes, I know," she said, snapping off Laurie's sentence.

"Well, it's cold right here by the door and they said you should come and sit by the kitchen where it's warm. They said they'd move. They said..."

She looked over to them. They huddled closer, easing their coats and scuffing their boots. There was no smirk there, and they didn't look up. Laurie stood hovering.

"It's warmer, really," she said.

She thought she shouldn't, but she didn't hesitate. She slid over in the booth and struck out her cigarette. Then she stood up, gathered her purse and her cup close to her and walked over to them. She felt the open bulk knit of her sweater and the movement of her body inside it. The men didn't watch her. They were silent and self-conscious, fussing with their spoons and turning their cups – heads down. She walked towards them, then behind them. They scraped their chairs forward, away from her, as she went by.

"Old Ben doesn't waste any money on heat."

The man was big in the face, with thick dark eyebrows. They were struck with gray and lay heavy over his eyes. They naturally deepened the lines that ran from their ends, two long creases down either side of his nose. She looked at him as he spoke. He had never been handsome and years of weather had left him entirely ugly. He smiled. His teeth were straight and even, and yellow. He pointed.

"Best seat in the house," he said.

Her eyes followed his fingers to a seat in the corner, next to the kitchen. It was half protected, beyond the curve of the counter. Now that her back was to them, she felt them watching her as she walked. She sat down. It was warm there. She felt it, touching at her, trying to cover her.

She sat half facing them, close enough to see them clearly. They weren't as big as she first thought, just bulky. They took up space. It closed her off from the rest of the café. Their great padded coats, their stuffing-filled vests; these men wore green and plaid and orange. They moved deliberately, like ponderous things, reaching slowly and holding firm and wide. She could hear their words, but their talk was even lower now, deeper from their throats. They leaned further over their table, closing the circle -- protecting themselves, and aware of her.

And she was aware of them -- the male of them, the thick parts, heavy with muscles, the smell of them, sweet dried oil, greasy fluids, things that splashed or dripped and stained their clothes. She noticed their hands, tight across the back with strong fingers and short nails. These were the hands that could move those great machines outside, warm them, spread their arms, make them reach, feel their vibration, the change in noise. Hold them trembling at the arc of their power -- make them work.

"You here on vacation, ma'am?"

Surprised, she twitched her head and refocused her eyes, looking for the voice.

"No," she said, "I'm here with my husband." As if a husband automatically made vacations impossible.

"Oh," the voice said, agreeing with her, "Not much to see this time of year."

"Too damn cold," said another voice

Many of the mutters agreed with that, and it was settled that it was indeed "too damn cold." Somehow she knew they meant it was "too damn cold" to be wandering around before dawn without a coat. She tried to think of something to say to them, some reason, some explanation of her presence. A plausible why. What could she say? I still like my husband but I just couldn't go back. I didn't know you were here. The orgasms next door drove me out. Instead she said, "It's a very nice area."

They liked that. Some of them leaned back in their chairs so she could look at them, and a couple of the younger ones even looked at her. She smiled weakly at them, softening, glad that they were pleased with her. She reached open her purse for a cigarette, conscious that she was nervous smoking and fumbled slightly, looking for her lighter.

"Ma'am," said the voice that had asked her if she was on vacation.

She looked up and found him standing right over her, with a lighter in his hand. It was poised on his thumb, flat and shiny. He flicked his wrist and it snapped open. The sound was sharp. She shook her head slightly, embarrassed by the intimacy of the gesture. He didn't move. She tilted her head back, looking up. His body covered her vision. She saw the tight plaid shirt across his belly and the big teeth on the zipper of his coat. Instinctively, she moved her face into his hand, and, with a firm snap, he burst the fire open. She felt the heat, saw the cigarette ignite, heard it burn. Then he closed his hand, and the flame was gone. For a second, all she could see was the fading afterglow of fire, dancing from his fingers. She stayed there, watching it, and then pulled her head back and took the cigarette from her mouth. She looked up into his face with her mouth slightly open, holding her breath before she blew out the smoke. His face was firm, scarcely traced with age, but his eyes were low and squinted. Then he turned away, the tail of his coat brushing across the top of her leg. She felt the weight of it touch her through her jeans and naturally tightened her calf up to it, then pulled her leg back, underneath her closing thighs, tucking her feet together and turning away. Over the heads of the men she could see lightness in the steamy windows, the sky thinning with morning, and she knew that because of the season, it was really quite late, and he'd be waking up soon. She wondered if he would worry when he found she wasn't there.

At the bottom edge of her vision, the bulk of them broke and the men moved, pushing their chairs and standing, pulling their cups up for a last swallow, adjusting their clothes and reaching deep into their pockets. And then there was money, flashing bills tossed out and confused stacks of coins clicking on the table. And they talked, louder, jostling their words at Laurie who came forward, her light voice twirling through their sounds, dancing on top of their deep voices as they herded around her. They liked her. One of them stopped, he spoke quietly and Laurie shrugged and tilted her head. He was younger than most of them, tighter across the hips, his great green coat newer, a corner tear, high on the shoulder, neatly sewn. He spoke again and Laurie laughed the high-pitched giggle of a child. He reached his hand out of his pocket and then looked quickly over his shoulder to the men funneling towards the door. He leaned forward but stopped abruptly and stuttered a glance back at her. She dropped her eyes away but too late, and the boy turned away from the girl and joined the men at the door. He stopped and looked back at Laurie, then hunched his shoulders to zip up the front of his coat and melted into the other men pictured in the fog window.

    She relaxed, sad because she had spoiled the kiss but glad that the men were leaving. She felt her shoulders droop inside her sweater and moved her legs out in front of her. The heat from the kitchen was warm and humid, and she reached a little into it. The last voices filtered through the café.

    "Don't think we can..."
    "What you waitin' on...fuel line..."
    "Woman like that'd...'

"Just damn cold...this year...same thing..."

And then there was silence. It was hollow -- not quiet but empty, like something had been taken away. Laurie gathered the money off the table. She stacked the cups as she went, scooping the change into her pocket and straightening the bills.

She watched and remembered when her life had been measured in dollars and dimes. She remembered the weight and value of them. How much care she had taken with the coins and how neatly she had arranged the bills. She reached for her purse.

"That's alright," Laurie said, holding a handful of money up for her to see. "Eddie said he'd take care of it."

She lifted her shoulders and gestured the question across the café.

"The one who lit your cigarette?" Laurie answered.

She smiled at the man's chivalry – misguided chivalry. "He probably makes less money than my secretary," she thought. Mistaken chivalry.

Laurie moved through the tables, fussing and straightening and collecting, slyly working her way around until she was practically beside her.

"Eddie's a nice one," she said to the rearranged stainless chrome combination napkin holder and salt and pepper stand.

"Him and George run the crew. George is the one invited you first." She continued wiping and talking.

"They been here all season, working on the bridge over at Dalton. Everybody says George is mean, but he's always been nice to me. They all have, 'cept Wendell, but there's something wrong with him. We were at a dance at the VFW and he just walked right in and started..."

Suddenly the empty wasn't good enough anymore. She didn't want to be stuck with Laurie, yammering away like they were friends. She missed the men, the idea of them, the purpose of them. Laurie's rambled-out words were little in the big room, lost just as they were spoken, useless time fillers continually reused until somebody else wanted a coffee or a doughnut and so gave Laurie her purpose.

"...Course he thinks he is," Laurie said shyly, looking over at the kitchen. "But he's awful young, really." She paused, "He doesn't know much about real life yet. Men are like that."

She hadn't been listening.

"They think they know everything but women really take care of things. You know, the real stuff. Men will be boys," she said happily, walking away.

What sophistication was this? Some gender-generated power struggle? A prenuptial risk assessment? When they married -- and they certainly would, baby-blue tuxedos, drunken groom and all – they'd have enough time for all that, and more. Their whole lives would be one endless cavalcade of "You did not." "I did so." complete with dirty diapers, greasy jeans and shapeless T-shirts. She sighed with her shoulders, ready to leave, but she didn't leave. She didn't want to leave.

Her irritation was completely real and entirely unreasonable. She knew that. No one had done anything to her. It came from nowhere. It was from the empty. She was tired. She was stuck – she was stuck with a low-end waitress in a shiny chrome café. She looked at Laurie. Actually, she wasn't that much older than the girl with the coffee cups, or was she? She had a car and a house and a yard and a secretary who brought her coffee and nodded approvingly when she bitched. She had stock options and credit cards and a hair stylist and a man sleeping in her bed. Laurie had an unraveled sleeve and six dollars in tips. She watched her bend over the table and reach forward to wipe it, pulling the waitress dress high on her legs and stretching it tight across her body, the green apron strings dangling and jolting with the rhythm of her movements. She wondered if Laurie was like the girl next door, shrill and urging and helpful when she made love to – had sex with -- the boy with the torn jacket. She wondered how he felt – young, strong and impossible to control. Laurie looked up and caught her looking at her.

"You want some more coffee or some breakfast or something?"

"No -- no food. More coffee, maybe?" she said, making it sound like a question, asking permission. Irritated that she sounded uncertain.

"I know what you mean. I just can't face food in the morning. 'Course I work with it all the..."

The door opened and Eddie and the boyfriend stood hesitating in the doorway.

"...time."

They walked towards her, moving through the tables. Eddie gestured to Laurie, who went over to stand with them. Then he took a few steps forward.

"Are you alright, lady? You got some trouble or something?"

She didn't answer, trying to decide what to answer. What could she say? Trouble? I'm cold and I wish I'd watered that stupid fern. You and your men like Laurie a lot. Do you notice I'm not wearing any underwear? Or maybe just "He's going to wake up -- eventually?" But all she said was --

"Chivalry."

"Ma'am?"

She sighed deeply, forcing her breath out, sagging her shoulders. She pulled her fingers through her hair, tucking it behind her ears, tidying it for the nice man. He was a nice man, who saw a woman -- or at least his version -- not a female, and she was stuck with that.

"Chivalry," she said again, "A much neglected concept." And she smiled at him.

"Ma'am?"

"Oh, well!"

She didn't know what to do. Outside the men were starting their machines, manipulating them, making them groan into life, the noise pushing into the room. She could almost see them, their hands on the gears, their feet braced against the pedals, adjusting their clothes, rubbing the windshields with their sleeves, coaxing, persuading, warming. And she felt the sounds of their response, deep and guttural, quickening from stuttering moans to one long, rumbling howl, slowly filling the room. He spoke again, louder and sharper, over the expanding noise.

"Look, I can't do nothin' right now 'cause I got the crew, but I can give you the kid here." He gestured back with his left arm. "He can get you where you're goin' and such,"

She looked at them, past Eddie, over his shoulders at the two young faces, wondering who they were and how Laurie and the boyfriend could possibly get her where she was "goin' and such" when they weren't going to get there themselves. And there, as if some unseen someone had wiped the fog from the windows, it became consciously clear to her. Nobody starts out as a waitress or a foreman or even an Account Manager for that matter. That's just where they end up. Her imaginings had been different. Her Barbie had been a lawyer and a veterinarian and a spy with a gorgeous apartment, tons of clothes and boyfriends -- plenty of boyfriends. Not a waitress or an Account Manager.

Eddie said something she couldn't hear.

But then things just get away from you – the line of it -- the great long line of it. Her house, her car, lunch, dinner parties, friends, recipes, wine, insurance, water coolers, water heaters, mutual funds, cell phones, primer, paint, portfolios, Peggy, Anita and Tom, Robert, his parents, Gerald from the bank and that goddamn fern forever dying in the corner -- all of it -- one continuous relentless stream. She had nothing she had ever wanted, nothing she would ever need. But how could she tell him that? He was just a nice man, a nice man who was offering her somebody else's boyfriend for the afternoon.

"You okay, lady?" he said or something like that.

No, it was all wrong. She wasn't a damsel in distress and shining knights don't come in plaid. She reached into her purse and pulled out a bill. She wasn't sure if it was a five or a ten, and it didn't matter, because now, there were even rumors of children. The final happily-ever-after broken. She dropped the bill on the counter and stood up, pulling her sweater down over her hips, feeling it drag across her naked nipples. And there they all stand, suspended in the loud. Eddie, uneasy, glancing between her and the door. Laurie concerned and unraveling in her off-orange waitress dress. The boyfriend, quiet with duty, the tear in his coat neatly sewn with careful small stitches that were nearly the same color green. And her, struck stupid, unable to understand or thank the nice man, simply because he wasn't the man she imagined he would be. She had no idea what she wanted to do, or even what she was willing to do, or what it would cost or what she would gain. She didn't know these people. She would never see them again, but somewhere Senior Account Managers made buckets of money. She looked directly at Eddie. She thought she would kiss him, take the three small steps she needed to get close to him, right next to him, so close he could smell her and then kiss him. Turn the plaid frog into a shining knight. A prince who would slay his own dragons and not pass her off to a secondhand teenager bespoken to a waitress. But even as she thought it, the unrequiting wants of her life bubbled up inside her, rising like some uncontrollable fluid and simply overwhelmed the needs. She stepped forward.

"Fuck off!" she said, solid and deliberately, throwing it into their faces as if it were their fault, the words thick and sticky and amoral. They didn't move, didn't react, her words drowned by the sounds of the men and their machines coming through the walls. Or did she just think it?

"Fuck off!" she shouted this time, violently shaking her hair out from behind her ears, "And leave me alone!"

She didn't wait, didn't look at them. She turned away and walked out, slowly, matter-of-factly, opening the door into the noise and the night. But it wasn't night. It was morning -- spreading everywhere, lighting the sky and overpowering the tiny last star bravely trying to twinkle. And the noise was palpable, touching her lips, vibrating in her belly, the roaring machines looming over her as she walked past them, fearless and crying, back to his car. Then she just drove away.

She woke him up when she came back into the motel room. They had breakfast and packed and went home. There were no explanations.

Several months later, hovering between life and death, the fern in the corner finally gave up and died, crisp and brown. They had two children in four and a half years. She quit smoking. Eventually, she did became a Senior Account Manager and never caught Robert sleeping with anyone. Her own infidelity with Anita's Tom ended badly and she never did that again. Somewhere they moved to a beautiful big house overlooking the river, but they never took another unplanned vacation, and for all the years her daughters were growing up, she never read them fairy tales.

------/\------

....The Dying of Daniel

She had decided the dying of Daniel was no big deal. She'd heard ugly rumors about it all spring from her mother, who, bored with her father's company, would telephone "just to say hello" and spread the usual gossip.

"He's not good, you know, dear," her mother had warned. But then, her mother was always warning her about something.

So the final telephone call was unexpected but no shock. Yet, between calling work, a minor shop when she discovered her assortment of little black dresses were all a little too little for a funeral and getting Jake and the boys combed, cooked and cleaned for a week, she did find she had tears. Middle of the night, kitchen table, glass of brandy tears. But then she put them away and was on the road the next morning.

The morning drive was pleasant, touring away from the sun with the windows full open and the music loud. She stopped at Butler's By the

River for lunch, just like they used to when the family made their annual pilgrimage to the cottage. Her childhood memories called it cleaner and a lot more elegant, but the food wasn't bad and it was cool on the patio. So she sat for a while over the river, nursing a reasonable second glass of wine.

Her mother had insisted on "sending your father down to get you" but she had been equal to it and equally insisted on driving herself. She was not so much afraid of being trapped by the parents, unable to escape, as being at their mercy, dependent on them. Now, looking around, she was glad. Despite it all, she liked her childhood memories intact, and a Butler's By the River, shabby and unused, didn't feel right to her.

The rest of the drive was hot. The endless heat of high summer that sweats at your throat and leaves you clinging to your underwear, damp and uncomfortable. So she was glad when she pulled off the highway and into the trees, remembering how cool it always was in the early evening by the lake. Peggy and Franklin, the couple formerly known as Mom and Dad, were waiting for her in the shade of the veranda.

"How are Jacob and the boys?"
"Fine. He's taken a few days off work."
"How was the drive?"
"Which way did you come?"
"That's a pretty skirt."
"Did you stop at Butler's?"
"No, I got a late start and whizzed right by." She slipped easily back into her childhood world of not so much truth.

"Do you want to clean up?"

"How about a drink? We're just having cocktails."

"A drink would be fabulous."

Frank, galvanized into action, retreated into the house and Peggy just kept talking.

"When is the funeral, mother?" Susan said, cutting through.

"Funeral?"

"Funeral!" She repeated gesturing.

"Funeral?"

"The funeral, mother!"

"He's not dead, dear," Peggy said, turning to put her glass down. "Of course, he's not good and Doctor Bates says….."

She sat or slumped back into the old wooden deck chair with one collapse of her shoulders.

"Mother, you told me he was dead. You distinctly told me – you said it. I'm sure you said it."

Peggy stopped talking and looked directly at her daughter.

"No, dear. You must have misunderstood."

"Oh, for Christ's sake!"

Frank, unaware of the conversation, arrived with the drinks just in time to salvage it.

"Sorry, we don't have your proper whiskey, Squeaks. You'll just have to make do with old Dad's Regular Rotgut."

Old Dad's Regular Rotgut was an expensive single malt and it tasted good. Susan turned away from her mother to the water. This was the time of day she always liked best -- the long pause between day and night -- and in the whiskey and the shade she relaxed into it.

"This was always such a nice place," she thought, as her annoyance with her mother drifted away on the breeze and faded into the fading light of the lake. And so they sat talking nothings, and watching the shadows stretch into the water.

"Well, drink up, Susan. We're all going to dinner with Fred and Teddy."

"Who?"

"The Aspinalls dear."

"Mother, I just got here. I'm tired "

"Now don't be contrary, dear. They'd love to see you and..."

"Hold it right there, mother."

"...Gerald's up for the funeral. You remember Gerald, dear"

"Ohhh, God." She remembered Gerald (never Gerry) a nasty spitball-headed kid with dirt under his nails.

"They're just dying to see you again."

"They don't even know I'm here, do they?" she directed the question at her father who didn't answer. "No, I'm going to have another drink and take a shower and relax for an evening. I haven't been here for years. I just want to veg tonight."

"Well, if that's what you think, dear, you don't have to come, if you don't want to, but we're going to our theatre group afterwards, and I imagine we'll be quite late."

So that was the plan – trap her into dinner and then an all-night session of showing her off to the neighbors.

"No, I'm fine," she said. "It'll be nice to have an evening to myself. What are you doing this year?"

"*Arsenic and Old Lace*," Frank answered, getting up to go. "I'm Theodore and your mother's handling the costumes again."

"I'm going to give it up after this one. It's getting just a bit too much for me," Peggy said, following Frank to the door.

"No, you're not," Susan thought. "You've been in little theatre since before we were born and you've done that stupid play a thousand times. What did we used to call it? Ass Lick and ... Ass Lick and..."

"You'll make a great Teddy Roosevelt, Dad," she said, hoisting her glass.

"Charge!" he said, opening the screen door.

"Charge!" he repeated, just inside the cottage.

Peggy stopped at the door and turned, "Peter's coming, you know," she said.

She didn't flinch, didn't move, didn't blink.

"And James?' Susan asked.

"I'm not sure about that. He and your father are fighting. He told me over the telephone -- it wasn't definite. I'll phone him again tomorrow." Peggy paused for a second and looked at her daughter, "There's plenty to eat, dear. You know where everything is." And then she was through the door, and twenty minutes later Susan was alone in the evening.

She finished her drink and watched the lake for a while, not troubling the several steps to the water. Later she scrambled some eggs and took a long, deep shower. Then she poured herself another whiskey, and, with her head wrapped in a towel, went back to the veranda. The night was still warm and sulky. The breeze off the lake touched at the trees and made them rustle like the sound of fingers moving curtains. The lights from the other cottages peeked and hid, in quick movements that she was only just aware of. They glanced off the tips of the waves in short silver scutters that disappeared in and out towards her in the darkness. And the shadows they made flickered at her, as if something was moving, and then something was. Somewhere close -- she could feel it on the back of her neck. For a minor second, she held her breath and searched, trying to quickly find it, tensing to go inside. Then, there -- at the lakeshore, he was walking, as if he'd been there all the time. And, of course, he had been. She just hadn't been able to distinguish him from the half-light, in the shifting trees. She knew his walk and watched him, a single shadow outlined by the lighter lake and the tiny lines of silvery cresting water. She knew he couldn't see her on the dark veranda, so she waited until he was facing her on the shore.

"Want a drink?" she said casually.

He twitched ever so slightly and she smiled. He didn't answer, so she got up and switched on the light. They could see each other clearly and she walked down and sat on the stairs. He lifted the can he had in his hand.

"I don't think so," he said, gesturing it towards the cottage.

"They won't be home for hours yet. It's little theatre night. When did you get in?"

"Just now," he said, taking a few steps from the shore to lean on the banister opposite her. "I parked at Champions and just came walking."

"You staying there?"

"Yeah, Tom's got it fulltime now. His dad's gone to Florida."

"Tom. I haven't seen him in years. How's he doin'?"

"He's okay. He and Sharon finally got married. They came down for a week over Christmas last year. I'm just returning the favor."

"They won't be pleased, you know."

He shrugged his shoulders and drank from the can.

"*They* have a full house with you and Jimmy and his bunch." He said.

"Jimmy's pissed with dad. Something about the business, I think."

"Jimmy's always pissed. He'll come. Mother'll make him. Where's your crew?"

"I left 'em at home. I decided this was going to be difficult enough without extra added attractions. Jake's got some time off."

He nodded in agreement and shook the can in his hand.

"Dad got anything worth drinking?"

She pointed her glass at the door behind them

"Old Dad's Regular Rotgut," she said.

He smiled at the old joke.

"You get it, Squeaks,"

"Oh, Jesus," she sighed. "Don't be childish, Peter."

He hesitated and then stepped forward onto the stairs, took the glass from her hand and crossed the veranda. The screen door bounced after him. She pulled the towel off her head, shook her hair loose and began to rub it dry. He came back out, set the glass down beside her and popped his beer can open with the other hand.

"You're going to have to deal with them eventually," she told him, through the towel.

"I'll see them at the funeral."

She stopped rubbing her hair and dropped the towel in her lap.

"He's not dead."

"What?"

"Nope, still in the land of the living. I didn't get it all, but he's very much..."

"God! If anybody can fuck it up, Daffy and Doris can."

They looked at each seriously for a moment and then started to laugh. It was an easy careless laugh that came from tension and comfort and years of memories, old jokes and fond mishaps -- just laughing, with every bit of humor they had ever shared over the years.

."She told me directly."

"Me too"

"Wrong guy?"

"Maybe she didn't have her glasses on."

And they laughed again. They knew it wasn't funny, but just between themselves they knew it was.

"We're terrible," she said, sputtering.

"She's going to have a gathering, you know. She'll beat him over the head if she has to."

"Mmmmmaa" she agreed, "I'd like to see that."

"Jesus! How do they do it? Every time?"

"I have no idea."

They sat quiet for a moment, giggling, exhausted.

"I gotta go, Squeaks."

"Yeah. Are you coming around tomorrow?"

He shrugged.

"I'll see you," he said and walked back into the darkness

She watched him go, silhouetted, the way he'd come, slowly disappearing into the darkness.

"Ass Lick," she shouted out towards the lake.

"What?" she heard faintly on the breeze

"Ass Lick," she shouted again, louder. "Arsenic and Old Lace? When we were children? What did we call it? Ass lick and what?"

He shouted back at her from the night, but he was too far away, and she couldn't hear him.

The next day was stinking hot. And the next. And the next. Or maybe there was just one. They all flowed together in one heavy, breathless mass. James was called and cancelled and cajoled and discussed to the ends of time. The cottage got smaller, shrinking into a stagnant stream of lounge and lunch. Flies droned and died and the white noise fans hummed on endlessly. She telephoned Jake and talked to the boys. She read her book and listened to her mother and watched her father going stale in the sunshine. Harassed, she went to the hospital but didn't manage to go in. She walked by the lake. Once, she abandoned her clothes and swam in Deadman's Cove and crawled up on Smuggler's Rock to stretch naked in the sun, finally cool and comfortable. Dreamy, she remembered the pirates they had fought there and the long, shady hot afternoons alone with their books and pencils and stories. It would always be 'Deadman's Cove' because Peter said it was and the name had become forever, but by then they didn't swim naked anymore. On 'Little Theatre Night' she waited on the veranda, but Peter didn't come back. So, on the third night, or maybe it was the fourth, she went to Champions.

Susan was amazed at the number of people there – practically everyone she'd spent her childhood summers with – a gang of teenage Hiawathas all grown up -- crowded across several tables and conversations.. They had all come back for the dying of Daniel.

But of course they'd come, she thought. He had taught them to do that -- along with how to swim, how to paddle a canoe, dive, table tennis, songs, games, all of it -- to do what was right, valuable and responsible.

"I didn't know you were here, Sue."

"Come, sit down."

"No, I just got in," she lied casually.

They laughed and drank and played 'Do you remember the time' and it was brilliant and fun. And everywhere, collected and bound, etched into brass trophy plaques and sealed in under-glass photos on the walls, were their childhood summers. She re-met Martin and Beverley who owned a card shop and Gerald (now called Gerry) who had clean fingernails and two kids, complete with pictures. He was a digital animator and worked with Peter. Where was Peter?

"Where did Tom get all this junk?"

"From the Rec Hall"

"I think he went off somewhere with Tom."

"God, Sue! I haven't seen you in ages."

"When Daniel got sick and..."

"Then Tom just brought it all up here."

In brief waves of alcoholic honesty, she could see Daniel there -- in them -- because of what he had really taught them: confidence and fair play, friendship, persistence, what is talent and how you use it, who goes first sometimes and how to wait your turn. All the natural virtues that parents can only hint at. A gang of savages transformed into genuinely nice people -- by Daniel.

"It's not like we didn't know..."

"...of course, he's only three, but they say it's never too early."

"And the great thing is nobody can tell the difference, unless you look really hard."

Apparently the party had been going on for days, or rather, nights. A bunch of overgrown teenagers re-trapped in their parents' homes, with nothing to do, void of responsibility, in an accidental family reunion. She learned the intricate connections, renewed her friendships, found the lost years, laughed and drank and sang, and even smoked a time or two, out in the trees behind the parking lot, where they used to.

"It wasn't the end of the world, but still.."
"Little Theatre Night …."
"I don't know, but he's awfully young."
"Remember Kumbayah?"
"Oh, God!"

They closed the place with old camp song sing-alongs, complete with rounds and solos and drunken pantomimes. Then they all walked home, down the same only road they all lived on, goodbyed with hugs and promises, until Susan was the only one left. The night was warm and smooth and the red sign said "Saint James" and she stepped over the same little fence, and the light was on in the trees to guide her, and she was fifteen again.

The next morning, she woke up fuzzy and throbbing. After a couple of hours of her father's good-natured teasing and Peggy's relentless joy in her reborn social life, she fled. Fled away to the lake and around it and up through the woods until she was back in the town and looking at the hospital. This time, she went in and bought a coffee and tried to drink it, and spilled it, and sat down on a wooden chair and stayed there, trying to control the sequence of events. She could not, and she knew it. The walls were green. They smelled of sickness and medicine. She sat there breathing, biting her lip and trying to escape, but she could not, and she knew it. So she asked at the desk and a pale green nurse told her #217. She went up the stairs and saw the door. It was open and she stopped and then stepped, and suddenly she was standing in the room, uninvited.

He looked dead, shining in the sunlight. An ugly angel preparing for God, his beautiful features destroyed by the sickness that ate through him. She saw this and was sad and didn't know what to do, so she stood there, helping him breathe.

"Daniel?" she said.

"Just barely."

He turned his head slightly and smiled at her, cheek hollow and ghoulish.

"Come sit where I can see you."

She hesitated.

"It's alright, Squeaks. I'm not contagious."

"It's not that... It's... not... It's..."

What could she tell him, now, after all these years and thoughts and mental conversations.

"It's... it's your hair," was all she could manage.

"The least of my worries," he said. "Come, sit. I want to see what you've become."

She sat straight in the metal chair next to him, the sun glowing through her, casting a deep shadow across the bed. She was aware of how she looked, hung over and pasty without make-up, her hair knotted, lank and dirty, her eyes red rimmed and bloodshot.

"You didn't have to dress up just for me," he said

"I ... I was at Champions," she said quickly.

"Ah, The Living Wake."

She looked pained.

"It's okay. I'm pleased that so many came back. It's important."

He took a long breath.

"It's important to see them again. See some result, some finish for me."

She sat, like a small animal caught in a brilliant light, unable to move. All the thoughts and words, questions and accusations, played out for years, over and over in the privacy of her own head, were caught now, trapped in her dry throat, blackmailed into silence.

"I wasn't sure you'd come," he said.

"I..."

"Is Peter here?"

She stiffened and lied.

"I haven't seen him."

He turned his head away from her, looking blankly at the ceiling.

"You used to be better at that," he said and turned his face back to her.

"Believe me, I just want to see him. I'm not looking for some final confrontation between us or anything. I've got the better memories and I'm holding on to them. Do you talk to him?"

"We see each other sometimes, but we don't talk. We could, but we don't. We got together once, years ago, but we spent the evening walking on eggs. It was bad, so...." her voice trailed off.

"So," he agreed sadly.

They sat silently with each other.

"It'll be over soon, Squeaks," he said kindly.

"Over?" she thought, "No, it's never going to be over. It'll drag on forever, like some unhappy cloud that darkens everything we're ever going to do. Haunting us for always. A half-dying secret, mournful and moaning. And for what! Nobody was hurt. Nobody needed to know. Everything was fine, just fine." And somewhere she wasn't thinking anymore. All the words from all the years, all the anger and hurt, trapped in that tight little ball of rage just exploded and came hissing and sputtering into the room. And she was speaking it all, loud and hard.

"Until you fucked it up. It was fine. Why? What possible reason? Who needed to know? Who were we hurting? Nobody! Then everything -- everything went to hell. What righteous, virtuous, goddamn...a - a - anything could do that?"

And she was crying and shouting and swearing -- mean with frustration, senseless with rage. And then the nurse was there and then an attendant and the room was full and loud and shouting and pushing her. And in it, the night came back to her, that same evil night -- just as real as it always had been, a thousand times had been. Peter and Daniel and Father, screaming at each other, in the kitchen, banging the tables and shaking the glass. Mother frantic, pounding on the door, shouting and raging at the lock. Jimmy, half slept and terrified, running back and forth, in his pajamas, howling. And crying and crying and crawling into the closet. Gasping for air in the breathless, mothball closet. Cowering in the corner, hands squeezed over her ears. Sobbing, and shaking, alone in the dark, pleading with God to make it stop. And she couldn't breathe and the sun stung her eyes and she couldn't see, and the attendant had hold of her arm, and she was fighting him away. And, and, and... And suddenly there was Daniel's voice, quiet and even, heavy with confidence and authority. The same voice she always knew. It parted everything. It told them to stop and listen, and they did.

"It's alright. It's fine." the voice said, "Susan, sit down, please. If we could get Susan a glass of water, maybe, and some tissues? There's some there. Just give us a few minutes, please. Thank you. Yes, it's fine. Just a few minutes. It's okay."

And, as if they were unruly children, he collected them to him and sorted things out.

Susan sat down, swallowed and sniffed and wiped the sun out of her eyes, not even hearing the words, just the voice of Daniel, controlling everybody else out of the room.

And they obeyed him. And then they were alone and silent, used up together.

"I'm sorry," she said finally. "It's just... I couldn't stop it. I'm so sorry."

"It's okay, Squeaks."

"No," she said painfully. "I should have..."

"I didn't know." Daniel said, "I really didn't know. I knew it was bad but I didn't know it was that bad. I remember things differently. I thought... I wanted to think... you understood, somehow. You, of all of us, could understand."

"I don't," she said. "I just don't. I trusted you...we...it...I. I can't...Why?"

She stopped, out of words, tired from it.

"I don't know," he said. "I did what I did, and I can't take it back. Maybe it was wrong. Seeing it now, I guess it was. But what was I supposed to do? Not see? Not feel?"

He stopped and sucked at the air.

"Surely you can understand that, Squeaks -- you of all of us. You know what it's like to ache, need, hurt with the want of it. Look what you were willing to do, just to touch, just to get close enough to touch."

It was still Daniel's voice, but it was hollow, labored and breathing. And all she could see was the bright white harmony of the bed, the sheets neatly tucked, the crisp pillows holding his head, the tidy folds drawing the lines of his body. A brilliant white sarcophagus, lying in the windowed sunlight, and her own deep shadow a single drama over it.

"But why?" she said, pleading.

"Why? There is no why. I wanted. I needed. I needed so much."

She reached forward and took his hand. It was bony and chilled. But she knew it was Daniel's hand, the one she remembered holding on to hers, keeping hers, while they sat, fingers crossed, when Peter took his driving test -- the hand that had helped her write 'Happy Birthday' on Peter's cake.

The one she trusted to tip the canoe in deep water -- the first time.

"I wanted. I needed. It was the only chance I had."

He curled his fingers around hers and held on.

"I am sorry, Squeaks."

She held his hand for a few seconds, quietly keeping it, until he fell asleep, exhausted.

The sad was like a stain, seeping, slow-motion brown and spreading. And every place it touched, it hurt, and she hated. Heartbroken, hated. The people in the street, the children laughing, the stupid sunshine dancing on the lake. Peter, for not being there. Her parents, her friends, even Daniel -- Daniel for dying. But mostly she hated herself – just her -- for not being good. A good person, someone she liked. Someone who would let a dying man die, someone who did the right things, on purpose, without thinking. She walked until she was tired, until she was past the cottage, until she was near enough to Deadman's Cove to go there. And so she did. She pulled off her clothes and plunged into the water, swimming off the taste of sickness and medicine. Diving deep to the bottom and then driving back to the surface to gulp air and do it again, and again, until she was too tired to do it again. Then, breathless, she climbed onto Smugglers' Rock and lay there face down, finally clean of it. And she daydreamed the day and memories of Daniel, and slipping in and out of sleep she dreamed them too. And finally, belly hot and hungry she swam back to find her clothes, go back to the cottage and wait for Peter.

Peter never came, but somewhere in the stuffy darkness, that night or was it the next, he telephoned, and she went to the hospital. And the three of them sat together again, while the parade of everyone came past them, pausing and leaving and coming back again, until they were all gone. In whatever hours there were that night, Peter never let go of Daniel's hand. And Susan never left them. And sometimes they talked together, and sometimes they didn't. And sometimes he held her hand too, and sometimes he didn't. And sometimes he knew they were there, and sometimes he didn't. And then, somewhere in the one lamp darkness, he just wasn't there anymore.

Two or was it three days later, they all came back, harnessed into their clothes against the hard heat of the summer afternoon. They stood on the lawn at St. James, slowly gathering their numbers until they spilled into the street.
"I didn't know he was Catholic."
"It's the dark one, one up from the corner."
"I didn't think he was anything. There wasn't any priest."
"Don't bother: he's obviously got his telephone turned off."
St. James was small, breathless and hot, dim and medieval after the brilliant outdoor sunlight. They stuffed themselves in, row after row, until the rest of them could only stand in the back. Susan

wasn't sure, but it looked as if some of them had been left outside. She and Peter and Jimmy sat up front, with Tom and Sharon and a couple of odd women who might have been aunts. The huge sun, streaming through the stained glass, cast dull pastel shapes across the floor, red and green and yellow, that tricked her eyes into the light and shadows, so all she could see were shades and silhouettes.

"We come together today to celebrate a life that touched..."

She felt the crowded mass of people behind her, felt the pressure of them pushing her forward towards the altar. All she could see were dull shapes that moved, faceless and dark, and the great golden crucifix, shining out over the gloom.

"...and surely we have no sorrow, for we have seen what Daniel..."

The droned voice and the heavy heat melted the shapes together until only the crucifix was clear, brilliant, shiny, filling her vision. And the breathing, crowding church pushed her, moving her up, over the coffin and the altar, floating her forward to embrace it. She saw the features of the Christ clearly, the look, painful rapture. She had seen it before. Long, firm muscles, hollow belly, smooth cloth bulging his loins. Sweat gathered under her arms and between her breasts, warm and clammy.

"... we know not what it is for us to be..."

She felt the weight on her, saw his face clearly, eyes half closed, mouth clenched. She felt the muscles in his back, his arms, her heels tucked behind his knees. Acceptance, possession, uncontainable strength, on her and around her, holding her. His face against hers, his breath on her throat. The half light dancing, the shadows in her unfocused eyes, moving, moving in the doorway, watching them. A featureless shade, silently watching them. -- seeing them grinding at each other, growling. And caught somewhere between girl and goddess, she didn't care. Her only existence was to make him melt into her, compelled beyond reason to shudder and quake, lost in holy ecstasy.

"Let us pray."

The church rose like bubbling oil. She felt Jimmy grab her elbow and pull her up to her feet.

"Heavenly Father, we come before You on this day to..."

And they prayed for Daniel and they prayed for themselves. And then someone sang, and Sharon read "If" until she couldn't stop crying. And then it was Peter's turn, his voice wet with emotion. But all she could do was sit, slumped in the sticky heat, until it was over and they all stumbled out, blinking, into their last endless summer.

Later, in the dark, the reception moved up the lane and across the street and turned into another party. Susan and Peter sat, knees up, on the curb in front of Champions, together alone, music and voices and everyone they knew and remembered, spilling from the inside to the outside and back again. Swirling around them. He poured her another drink from the bottle on the sidewalk.

"Wine?" he questioned, after her glass was full and the bottle was empty.

She smiled, "God, what a week. Has it been a week? Has it been any time at all?"

"Ahh-ahh-ahh," he exhaled, shaking his head. "Mother talk to you yet?"

She shook her head, shrugging it off.

"She got me in the churchyard."

She looked up at him blankly and he laughed.

"Well, Squeaks. It seems Daniel was quite the businessman. Apparently, way back in the day, he incorporated himself, the Rec Society, the Marina, the campsites, the beach, etc. etc. etc. and the fact is, Camp Counselor Daniel actually owned this town."

She opened her hands in front of her and Peter looked up from his drink.

"He left it all to us. Everything -- right down to the last blade of grass. Apparently, Squeaks, we're rich." he said ruefully.

"Why?"

"Why do you think?"

He raised his glass and touched the stem to the rim of hers. It made a light tinkling sound, like a Christmas bell. It remembered something in her, and she shivered.

"Here's to you, Daniel, old boy," he said and drank, finishing the glass.

She watched him look up and, without any effort at all, conjure another bottle out of the crowd, saw him reach up with his hand and gesture, twitching his fingers, self-assured, impossible to deny. Then with a minor grimace and a slight shake of his head, end the conversation and seal them up again.

"You do that like you were born to it," she said.

"I own this town."

They smiled together and sat with each other for a moment – quiet in the middle of all the people and music and voices.

"What happens now?"

"About what?

She didn't know. She didn't have frames for her questions. She didn't have questions. She did - but – but what – what do you say when you discover that the truth doesn't matter, and people die whether you're nice to them or not and when things are gone, they're lost and just because you feel a thing it doesn't mean you fixed it?

"Did you sleep with him, Peter?"

"Once," he said and paused to take a drink. "Twice, actually. I don't count the first time."

She looked.

"It was that night after all the shouting and everything. We went back to his place. It's not like I had any place to go. We drank wine, quite a lot of it… and… well… there was a lot of tension that night."

"The same night! The same bed! God, men are pigs!"

"I knew you'd understand, sister dear," he said, and they laughed – laughed together - like the first night. Like when they were children. Like normal.

"I didn't know," she said finally, "Didn't know until I talked to him. God, was it just a few days ago?"

He shrugged.

"It was more for him than me. It's not really my thing. We stayed in touch for a while but it just... it just faded away."

"You left me that night," she said seriously

"I know. In all of it, it's the one thing I do regret."

"What about the parents?"

"Ah, You got custody of them."

They stopped again.

"We've never talked about it. Do we need to talk?" she asked.

"I don't know. What do you say? Things happen. We can't take them back."

"I just think I should feel differently."

"You feel what you feel, Squeaks. You can't manufacture the way you feel."

"Yeah, but..."

"Look, are you a bad person? Do you have green saliva? Beat your kids? Kick the dog? Steal? No. You're not warped. You don't write your telephone number on Men's Room walls."

He paused.

"Do you?' he said, smiling.

"Of course not."

"Well, neither do I. And I don't expose myself to little girls in the park, either. Face it,

Squeaks. We tried our best to fuck it up, but in the end we turned into decent human beings."

"But that's just it; I don't think I should've. I should feel some...something, but I don't. I don't feel sorry -- not at all. I feel worse for Daniel. All those years. It must have been terrible for him. I didn't know. Maybe I..." she said, her throat closing on the words.

"What are you looking for, Squeaks – guilt, or absolution?"

"I don't know. Both, I guess, but I really don't want either."

"What is it you do want?"

"Normal! God, are we ever going to be normal?"

"Normal? Normal just happens," he said, "There's nothing you can do about it. Today, this is normal but tomorrow will be too. We're gonna get up and drive home and get back to doing whatever it is we do and forget all about this again. Jobs, house, kids, shopping. That's normal. We adapt. Life goes on."

"Yeah, I guess. I'm just glad it's finished. I'm sorry he's dead but.... it feels like it's over and I'm glad. Daniel told me that. He said it would be over." She looked up into the middle distance over Peter's shoulder.

"Daniel knew what he was talking about." Peter said sadly. "He always did."

"You know," she said, looking down and toying with her glass, "I saw him that night. Saw him in the doorway and I didn't do anything. I didn't stop it. I didn't want to."

"Yeah," Peter said evenly.

He steadied himself with his hand and stood up.

"C'mon, Squeaks." He smiled big, with crinkly eyes. "Let's get a canoe and give him a proper funeral."

He reached down, offered his hand and pulled Susan to her feet.

"It's the least we can do," he said, looking down into her face.

And they set off, dragging the crowd along with them, Peter sweeping them along, just like he always could, explaining as they went. Tom had the keys to the marina and the three of them pulled out a canoe. They stuffed it with everything and anything and everyone joined in and they doused it with vodka or whiskey or something and set it on fire. And then they launched it out into the lake, just exactly the same way Daniel had taught them. And as it floated out into the current the flames suddenly caught the breeze and roared against the sky, snapping and crackling and dancing on the water like a fiery soul reaching for heaven. And they all cheered madly -- a primitive tribe facing extinction. And they cheered Daniel. And they cheered themselves. And they danced across the beach and drank and sang long into the night, playing like the children they would never be again. And Susan, caught in the mess of them milling and talking and shouting, grabbed Peter and held onto his arm and they found Jimmy and hugged him tight to them. And Susan knew it was over.

The next day she started late, the car loaded with gifts and food and mother hugs and father advice. Jimmy promised Thanksgiving this year, maybe, and nobody mentioned Peter. She drove back through the town, but on a hot summer day everything but the beach was quiet and empty. She stopped at the cemetery, just to sit in the car for a moment. The dying of Daniel had been a big deal, after all. Then she drove past Champions, and saw Tom and Sharon cleaning up the mess, but Peter's car was gone so she didn't stop. She just drove by, turned onto the highway and headed home. Home to normal -- whatever that included. What had Peter said, 'jobs, house, kids, shopping?' That's about it. He was right; normal was just going to happen. Of course, she and Peter would have to deal with the estate at some point. Maybe they could talk about it, some weekend after things settled down a bit. Jacob could take the boys to his parents. They loved going to their grandparents. Some weekend would be good. Susan turned up the music and drove home.

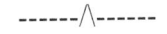

------/\------

....The Last Romance of Jasper Conrad

It was deep in the season. It was going to be hot, summer folding over itself like thick white chocolate pouring from a bowl. For now, the sun, slow and luxurious, filtered through the trees in sparkled shades of green and -- was it citrus or gold? Where the breezes were, light, like little silver fairies, danced and played, chasing themselves across the paving stones and into the garden. At least, that's how he saw it.

He sat on the edge of a neat row of starched breakfast tables with his back to the hotel. He drank his coffee and looked out into the trees and down the broad stone steps that led to the sand and the sea. In the color and shadow he couldn't tell what was light and what was movement, so what he thought he saw, he didn't actually see -- at least, not until the top half of her seemed to rise out of the blue water. She stepped up the stone steps and stopped at the top, dropped her shoes, and awkwardly, one-leg pretty, tried to brush the wet sand off her feet. Then she saw him. She stood straight. She picked up her shoes and walked toward him and the hotel. He was the only one there, and she chose a table a respectable English distance away from him. He thought about it for a moment, measuring the still light and the fresh quiet air. Then he closed his book.

"They're not open yet," he said, loud enough for her to hear. "It's too early."

She turned her head.

"I have coffee if you like?"

She looked directly at him, pausing that universal female nanosecond. Weighing the invitation – acceptance and consequence. Divining his purposes and his intent and calculating her own interest, plus or minus the inconvenience.

Instantly, instinctively, she knew he spoke American English. He was neatly dressed, his face was alive and he smiled, he was older (not father-ish but certainly not a proper sexual partner) and he was only offering coffee. But still, there was something...

He reached across the table and turned a cup over onto its saucer. She noticed it was opposite him and smiled. She decided, gathered her bag and shoes, put on a serious face, walked over, and sat down, all in one deliberate motion.

"Thank you," she said shooting her hand across the table, her arm stiff and her fingers slightly wide. "My name is Frances, but everybody calls me Sissy."

"Older sister?" he asked.

"Three," she said. "And you are?"

"The older brother."

He took her hand slightly and wagged it.

"Huh! What? Oh, sorry, I meant your name."

"Jasper Conrad, pleased to meet you."

"Thanks for rescuing me," she said, pouring coffee for herself and offering him more. "I simply can't survive without coffee in the morning."

He nodded for her to pour.

"How did you manage this?" she asked, sweeping her hand over the table.

"Oh, I bribe the help. That dapper-looking fellow over there is my housekeeper's brother, or cousin or something. I tip him outrageously"

"You're not at the hotel?"

"No, but I assume you are."

"Yeah, we flew in last night. The plane was late, and with the bags and time and everything, I really haven't gotten much sleep."

She said it as if it should to be important to him, perhaps the reason she accepted his invitation. But she was tired, her face tugged with sleepless lines that touched red at the bottom of her eyes.

"Still working on North American time?"

"Rome, actually. We came from Rome. It's not jetlag: we've been in Europe all summer. I just -- couldn't sleep. So I got up early and went for a walk. I love mornings. It so beautiful and quiet when the world's still asleep. Don't you think?"

She didn't pause.

"Then everybody gets up and starts charging around as if it matters. Televisions and cars and –

ah – I don't know. Nobody takes any real time to enjoy things. Just simple stuff…"

He listened without hearing, just as sympathetic as he always was when he heard clichéd bullshit.

"What do you do?"

It took him a second to realize she was talking to him again.

"Nothing," he said, as if it were a profession.

"Nothing?" she questioned.

"Nothing." He shook his head. "What about you?"

"Law. Well, actually, not really. Not yet, anyway. We're still students, but this is going to be our – uh – Tony's last year."

"Business law?"

"Corporate law," she corrected. "What do you mean you don't do anything? Everybody does something."

"No, not really," he said, holding his cup in midair.

"What would you like to do?"

He could feel her gathering up her TV talk show "You can do whatever you want" speech. It was cute, and so he didn't laugh.

"Nothing." He raised his index finger straight up. "That's why I'm doing it."

She smiled vaguely.

" Honeymoon?" he pointed.

"Not yet," she said, waving her left hand fingers in the air. "Well, actually, we almost got married in Rome. But it was just too complicated. It would have been fun, though. We decided to wait until at least one of us articles and we're a bit more established."

"How does that work?"

"Well, quite simply, you get a placement in a law firm. You get exposed to the actual workings of the law. Practical experience combined with an opportunity to…"

She sounded serious again, so he cut her off.

"Slaves from the university?"

"I suppose," she laughed. "That's why we're here. The next few years are just going to be a total grind."

She made an offhanded gesture to indicate everybody knew that.

"So we decided to take this summer off and just relax and travel and see Europe."

"Good idea. Bit of an adventure before the storm."

"Mmm, yeah, I guess." She spoke tentatively, looking around.

"You don't like Europe?"

"I like it alright," she said, pausing long enough to sip her coffee. "Actually, I can't really tell. It's not exactly as advertised, is it?

"No, not really," he agreed, tactfully.

"The sights are good and everything, but man is it ever crowded! Everything takes so long. We spend most of our time standing in line or waiting around to stand in line. And then when you get there, it's no big deal."

"You see one Mona Lisa, you've seen them all," he offered.

"Yeah," she agreed, clearly not listening.

"And everybody's always talking about the food and the wine and how great it is. The stuff we've had is pretty ordinary. It's good but..." her voice trailed off, "It was brilliant here this morning though, down by the water. They sweep the rocks with these big long brooms and rake the sand."

He liked this woman. She was fresh: the clichés were all still real to her, but she didn't enjoy them. She wasn't a fool, or at least wasn't going to be fooled for long.

"The thing is Europe's huge and there's all kinds of places I think I haven't seen. Uh – I don't know. I guess I was expecting something different."

"Is this your last stop?"

"Yeah – uh – no. We've got another week in London."

"London's nice. I've spent some time there."

As they spoke, or rather she did, things were moving around them. The light was changing, the sun getting higher over the trees. He could see it reflected in the big dark sunglasses perched in her hair. The seabirds were gone, and the silence they left was being broken by small voices and the tink touch of dishes. There were people gaggling out of the hotel in twos and threes, looking and adjusting, expanding their presence, filling the air, until....

"There's Tony."

He looked away from her to where she was looking.

"The green shirt is Tony, and that's Elizabeth and Foster."

Instead of waving to them, she got up to go.

"Thanks for the coffee. I hope you don't think I'm just a nasty bitch."

"No problem. I'm open every morning."

She stepped away.

"Hey," he said, loud enough to make her turn around, "Don't let the bastards grind you down."

She smiled and walked away.

"Where were you?"

"I just got talking to some guy that lives around here somewhere. I think he said his name was Jesse or Joseph or something."

They stopped to look at her.

"He speaks English!"

That didn't help.

"Oh, for God sake."

The next morning was the same morning, warm and promising hot. She walked along the moving water, trailing her toes in the dog-yellow sand. He stopped to buy a newspaper as he sometimes did and talked with Cosmenco. Then he walked to the hotel. He ended up at the same table, but she had gotten there first.

"I bribed the help," she said, offering him his table with a flick of her open palm.

"I see," he said, sitting down. And he did see. She was much more polished this morning: more make-up, clearer features, brighter eyes, neatly tucked in and unwrinkled.

"I think I may have given you the wrong impression yesterday," she said, waiting for him to agree. "Ugly American tourist?"

"Not at all. I thought you were refreshingly honest. And you said an awful lot of nice things, too, even though I'm sure you think they're all crap."

She paused slightly in mid pour. This was not the mental conversation she'd had with him the night before.

"How do you know what I'm thinking?"

"I have a very fine-tuned nose for bullshit," he said, reaching for the coffee pot.

"Apparently," she snapped. "So, okay then: what do I think?"

He looked at her. She was obviously used to people agreeing with her and didn't like it when they didn't. Morning coffee with a tousled Venus rising out of the water was one thing, but a petty quarrel with a sharp dressed wanna-be lawyer was quite another. He arched his eyebrows.

"I don't really care," he said, leaning back. "In a couple of days you're not even going to exist. You're going back to wherever it is you come from, and life will go on."

She looked at him.

"Okay, okay. I'm sorry. I just didn't want you to think I was a flake. I came to apologize."

"Apologize?"

"I feel bad. I just wanted to say I'm sorry."

He looked puzzled.

"I've been living out of a suitcase for a couple of months, and I'm edgy and irritable. You were the first person that seemed to care, so I just started talking. I didn't mean to dump on anybody." she offered her apology with an open palm.

"You didn't dump on me -- or anybody else, as far as I'm concerned. Look, we had coffee and a conversation. What are you? The American ambassador?"

This was not going well, at all. All the well-shaped phrases and witty responses she'd constructed in her mind through dinner and drinks the night before were useless.

"You don't like Venice. Big wow! Neither do I. It smells." He found himself enjoying himself. "And the food isn't that good, either. Certainly not as good as Florence."

"We didn't go to Florence," she said.

"The food's better. You shoulda gone."

She looked pained.

"It's just -- I've been having such a crappy time, and you were so nice to me I felt bad about being such a bitch. It's just – I'm sorry, okay?"

He could see that she meant it. She really thought she'd been nasty. He smiled to himself at the size of her ego.

"If that's the best you got," he said shaking his head, "It can't be all that bad."

"Oh, it isn't, I guess. It just seems like the whole time's been wasted. I thought we were going to come to Europe and have fun and do things. Find neat little places and meet people. Just hang out and enjoy it. We haven't done anything like that. We've just been typical tourists."

He didn't know what to do. Obviously, he'd opened up some personal Pandora's box, and this rant was what was coming out. She was a spoiled brat, upset about not getting her own way, but he didn't think to shut her up. He liked her. He listened and waited.

"I've been pushed around all summer. I've stood on my head, craned my neck, tried my best -- and for what? All we've done is tick the tourist boxes like it's a fucking shopping list."

She pronounced the 'g' in fucking, never a good sign.

"Buy the t-shirt, eat the spaghetti, ride the donkey. I've seen people -- this is true -- people taking pictures of pictures hanging on the wall. Yeah! And then showing them to the people standing right beside them -- right there. You should have seen them in Paris. Assholes! Yesterday we spent all fucking day on pots -- broken pots, smashed all to hell, and bones, and like little bits of trash that could have been *anything*. Then you go read the thing, to find out what it's supposed to be, it's in like eight different languages like it's all so-o-o important. If I see one more pile of rusty fucking junk, I'm going to scream. That's it!" She took a breath.

"I see you have discovered your inner bitch."

"Doesn't Europe have anything *real*? With like people in it? Real living people?" It's like Disney World on steroids out there. Nobody's going to tell me these people run around in wooden shoes and funny hats all the time. They don't. I'm sure they don't."

"Quit going on the tours," he said, matter-of-factly, stopping her in mid harangue. It was a radical concept she hadn't thought of, and, exasperated, she sank back in her chair.

"It's all part of the package," she said, giving up.

"So what?"

He reached for the coffeepot.

"They don't care if you show up or not. I assume you've already paid for all this. Just don't go. Take…"

"You're Jasper Conrad!"

The voice came from directly over her shoulder. Jasper looked up. It was Tony, the boyfriend from the morning before. Jasper recognized him and stood up.

"You must be Tony," he said.

"Wow, Jasper Conrad! This is great. How totally weird!" He turned back to his two-man entourage, presumably, Elizabeth and Foster. "It's Jasper Conrad."

They looked at him.

"He played lead for Vexxation."

Nothing.

"Lead guitar!"

He made air guitar motions with his hands but they were still blank.

"This is so weird," Tony said, turning his head away from the philistines. "What are you doing here? In this place?"

"Nothing," Frances said.

They both turned to look at her and she folded her arms, tilted her head and stuck out her tongue.

"How? How do you know me? You're way too young for Vexxation."

"No, I grew up on you guys. My step-mom is just a huge fan. They played 'Vertical Bedroom' at their wedding. This is so weird. She is gonna freak. Wow!"

"At their wedding?"

"Yeah." Tony nodded his head knowingly..

Frances stood up. She pulled her bag all the way up to her shoulder and kicked on her sandals.

"We have to go," she said.

"Yeah, right. Can I get an autograph for my step-mom? She just..."

"Sure," Jasper patted his chest. "I don't have a pen."

Foster stepped forward. "Just a sec. I'll get a ...."

"I need breakfast."

He gestured to Frances with his hand. "When are you guys coming back to the hotel today?"

"We're here all day. It's a free day. We're just going to hang out." Tony looked around for confirmation. Everybody seemed to agree.

"I'm actually starving."

"Just two minutes!"

"I'll tell you what: I'll come back at lunch and sign something for you then. How's that?"

"That would be great."

"Say about noon?"

"Could we get some food now?"

"Oh, and I don't broadcast – you know."

"Yeah. Right." Tony touched his finger to his lips, "Great! I'll see you then."

Frances had already walked away before they made their 'pleased to meet you' good-byes.

"Who is that guy?"

"He's this old rocker dude. They had this gihugic band back in the day. They were big, like massive. Dad and Sheila saw them at the Superdome or in like California. I forget. But they were *big*. They had like videos awards, Grammys, all kindsa crap -- movies. Then they go up onstage in Tokyo or Shanghai or someplace like that, and they have this major fuckin' meltdown, right there in front of like eighty thousand people! They just start wailing away on each other, right onstage -- cops and everything. Sheila had it on video, but it's gotta be on YouTube. Absolutely hilarious."

They caught up with Frances.

"Seriously, Sissy! You totally know how to pick 'em. Anyway, they break up the band, but a couple of years later they try to get it back together, but it's totally fucked at this point. They did some concerts, but they're all like so wasted they don't have a clue what's going on. Passin' out in interviews, shit like that. They called *this* guy," Tony gestured behind him, "Jasper the Disaster."

"What band was this? How come I never heard of them?"

"Vexxation! You know. They did that dicky thing with the two x's on the CD covers. You know la la, la, la la la la, la la la, la la la," Tony said, singing the chorus.

"Oh, yeah. From the car commercials"

"Yeah, that's them, Vexxation."

"What's he doing here? He's got to be totally rich."

"Fuck, Foster. I don't know. Why don't you go ask him? Old guy just hanging out, I guess. He's probably so brain-dead he doesn't know where he is."

"Tony, you can be such an asshole, sometimes." Frances said, sitting down again.

"What?"

They spent the morning playing on the beach like children, sunshine and sandcastles. Then, at noon, they dutifully trooped back to the restaurant for lunch. Jasper was waiting for them. He was different -- bigger, more animated. Frances sat directly across from him, watching him shine, perform, play with them. He made them laugh, and encouraged their stories, giving them each a chance to shine. It was audience participation and they got their money's worth, with pictures to prove it. Then, like some smiling gypsy merchant, he reached into his bag.

"Here, I think your mother might like these."

He handed Tony a CD.

"That one's *Cannery Rogue*," he said. "Don't break the seal. It has all our signatures on it. We signed a couple of hundred of them at the factory before they put them together, so it's definitely authentic. This one..." he popped the back off the other case, "is *Flexible*. It's got "Vertical Bedroom" on it. What's your mother's name."

"Step-mother. It's Sheila."

"To Sheila: Sorry I missed the wedding." He mouthed the words and signed it with a flourish. "How's that?"

"Great, I thought you'd just like sign a napkin or something. Thanks so much. She's gonna just vibrate when she sees this."

"No problem. I have to go now. You guys enjoy."

He stood up and looked directly at Frances, down at her. She felt like he was seeing her personally, like she was to blame for this, and now he had a claim on her. She owed him. This was all going horribly wrong.

The afternoon was long and silky. Tony and Foster rented jet-skis, loud and shouting, and tore out over the water, fading their noises into the distance. Elizabeth flirted with the rental boys, playing with her hair and chewing her fingers in adolescent sexy, and then she bought a hat. Frances lay in the heavy sun with her book, good to be on her own, reading and not reading, wandering thoughts, warm and half asleep. Sometimes, she followed the words, but she didn't really care who killed Chester Manville anymore. Mostly, she just looked at the dark tint sunglass sky, all of her alone, hopelessly bored in the crawling hours until morning.

"You need to cover for me. I've got this thing."

Frances turned out of herself to Elizabeth.

"Just say you forgot something, and I'll go get it for you. Not really. Like -- find it five minutes after I'm gone or whatever."

"You can't keep doing this, Libby. Foster's gonna find out."

"I just need like 20 minutes -- not even."

Frances looked up at her friend.

"Have you seen him? He's totally hot. I think his name is Brunoesco or Bruchesco or something."

"Are you kidding? If I say I forgot something, Tony's gonna go."

"Not if it's tampons."

"Forget your own!"

Then she stopped. It was perfect, almost perfect. It would work -- at least, for a little while. Maybe?

"Okay, but this is the absolute last time. Promise?"

"Promise."

It did work, brilliantly. Elizabeth didn't even miss the main course at dinner; the only casualty, sand in her hair and her underwear. Frances spent the rest of the evening rehearsing.

Like the same morning before, it was the same morning again. She didn't walk by the water, but she was there, at his table, waiting, and she poured his coffee when he walked in.

"You're getting to be a habit," he said, sitting down.

"Good or bad?"

He shrugged.

"I just wanted to say I'm sorry for..."

"Of course you are." He stopped her with his hand in the air. "What? Do you just wander around the world, apologizing for whatever crosses your mind? You're like some demented puppy that keeps peeing on the floor."

"That's not very nice."

"No, it isn't, is it?" he exhaled, "Let's do this. Let's have a conversation that doesn't start with 'I'm sorry.' Now, what's on the agenda today?"

"Nothing," she said, bright and pleased with herself. "I'm taking your advice."

"Huh?"

"The tour's going up the coast to this authentic," she made a quote sign in the air, "market to shop or whatever, then over to some ruins and dinner. But I'm not going. I'm officially sick."

It was all bound together with square-shouldered teddy-bear defiance. For the first time, he couldn't help it and he laughed -- out loud -- and felt terrible about it.

"Now *I'm* sorry," he said, "I didn't mean to laugh, but of all the junk around here, the ruins are actually worth seeing."

"Yeah, right. Six hours on a bus with an open bar and some drunken fucking Bulgarian Luau at the end. No thank you."

"Suit yourself. What have you got, anyway? Nothing contagious, I hope."

"You're making fun of me."

"No, I'm not. I'm just wondering what you're doing. When I said don't go on the tours, I didn't mean dump your friends. You want the real Europe. What's wrong with taking a walk through the town? It's right over there." He waved offhandedly.

She looked entirely deflated. This was not going very well.

"God! I can't win here," she said, opening her palms. "And why didn't you tell me you were famous?"

"What?"

"You could have told me."

"Hi, my name's Jasper, and, FYI, I'm famous?"

"You know what I mean."

"Look, I keep a pretty low profile. People don't recognize me all that often, but when they do, it usually ends up something like yesterday."

"And that's what I'm trying to say sorry about."

"You - didn't - do - it," he answered, measuring his tones

This was ridiculous. He didn't know this woman. He didn't owe her anything. But it was all out of control. She was genuinely sorry for something, but whatever it was, it was just making them both angry.

"And all this bullshit about I don't do-o-o-o anything."

"Hold it!" he said, stopping her, "You've obviously got a problem here -- with s-s-something. I don't know -- but I'm not involved.

You want to sit and bitch about your vacation, fine; I'm here. Knock yourself out. You want some weird, incoherent argument about nothing, you've got a perfectly good boyfriend sleeping it off upstairs. Have a go at him." He hunched his shoulders. "What is it you want, anyway?

"Why does this always go so badly between us?" she said, asking.

It wasn't rhetorical, but he didn't know how to answer. There was no reason. There was no "us." They were strangers. Yet they had become attached somehow to this bizarre set of recurring circumstances, and now they couldn't disentangle themselves. The Ancient Fates, watching and laughing and refusing to cut the yarn. He could see he had hurt her -- accidentally but *really* -- and he wasn't sure how or why he was going to fix it. But he did feel bad about it, and that was real also. Along with the damn sun moving madly across her sunglasses, and her wilting eyes looking around to gather up her things and leave, the sounds of the hotel coming to life, the skipping gurgle of tourists talking in the distance. Time moving on -- not stoppable enough to do him any good. He liked this woman but certainly not enough to fight with her. So he just did the next best thing, and her only objection was.

"I've got to be sick until their bus leaves."

Two hours later, they were walking along the broad boardwalk that separated the line of tourist beach resorts from the town. The nightspots and neon, shoddy and gaudy in the midmorning sun, were already out and open, looking for another day. There were a few strains of thump bass music hanging in the air and a couple of early partiers lizarding in the sun, but neither one of them noticed. Near the end, they stopped at Cosmenco's and he introduced her. Then they went down the three plank steps into the old town. He had convinced himself that he was simply going to be the tour guide, and after that, she was on her own.

"This is Europe," he said, waving his hand forward, "That's the Black Sea. Behind you is every resort known to man. The locals call it Legoland. In front of you, if you go far enough, is Istanbul. That's Pabrovo's bread and cake shop. There's Nick the butcher or something-- uh -- anyway, dead animals, and that monster way over there is the Orthodox church. How we doin' so far?"

And so they walked into the day.

"Roustov, there," he pointed, "waters the fish. It makes it heavy, no true weight, but he gets the earliest catch. It's fresh, but he's scamming you"

"You know everybody."

"This is my neighborhood," he said, spreading his arms. "Besides, most of them are related to my housekeeper. But don't get too carried away: these aren't their real names. I have no idea what these people are actually called. I never learned the language beyond hi, good-bye and where's the toilet?"

"How long have you been here?"
"I don't know. I don't remember. Years."

The people they found were bright and busy, but everyone seemed happy to see them, and they stopped to talk several times. But it was really just the two of them walking along. Amusing stories and all the usual questions.

"Some people say Roxolana came from around here."
"Should I know her?"
"No, she was a Turkish Sultan's wife."
"Are you married?"
"Not anymore."
"Do you have any children?"
He laughed.
"There's a couple of young people who get in touch when they need money, but mostly they live with their mothers."
"Mothers?"
He let that one pass.

Some of the streets were away from the sun, shaded refuges with uneven sidewalks and untidy gutters, but they didn't really notice.

"Why law?"
"Believe it or not, it's fun. Tony wants to go places with it, but I like the *doing* of it -- the intricacies. It's like a giant word maze." She moved her hand in the air, following an imaginary

path. "And then, when you get it right, it's such a total buzz."

"I've never had much luck with lawyers."
"You just haven't met the right ones."

That's how they spent their day, walking and talking until they ended up, late in the late afternoon, at a patio restaurant, tucked in between an ornate old apartment building and the sea. The place was practically empty and they sat, by themselves, at the end of a long wooden table.

"What you want, lady?"
"This evil-looking gentleman is Ferguson. He's says he's Scottish, but I have my doubts." Jasper leaned in for a stage whisper, "I think he's a gypsy."

It was an old inside joke.

Ferguson bent from the waist and gently lifted Frances' hand up to his lips in a courtly kiss. Frances smiled, but before she could say anything he turned her hand over and squeezed the flesh at the base of her thumb between his knuckles. It wasn't hard enough to hurt, but it startled Frances and she pulled her hand back.

"Oww!"
"Dobur," Ferguson said and nodded at Jasper. He turned back to Frances.
"So, what you want, lady?"

Frances rubbed the sting in her palm and looked around.

"I don't know. Do we get menus?"
"No menus. Ferguson only serves seafood. He goes down to the harbor every morning and

buys whatever he thinks looks good. Then he cooks it the way he likes it. That's it. The only choice you get is large or small. But he claims it's the best in town.

Ferguson looked on expectantly.

"But I don't know what we're doing. Is this dinner? Are we finished?" Frances shook her head between the two men, "Do I have to save room? Help me out."

Jasper laughed.

"You're funny. Don't you even want to know what it is? Most people want to know what they're eating before they worry about serving size."

Frances stopped and looked directly at Jasper.

"Well, I assume you haven't brought me all this way just to poison me."

Jasper tilted his head, like a question perhaps only to himself. Yes, he did like this woman. In a world of prefabricated females, she had her own personality. Maybe it came from her soaring ego, but so what? Her thoughts were honest -- at least as far as she recognized them, anyway. And they had had a pleasant day just walking and stopping and talking. Jasper had enjoyed showing off, and she seemed genuinely pleased with the day he had given her.

"When do you want to go back?" he said.

"I don't," Frances shrugged,

Jasper thought about it for a few seconds and stood up.

"Not today, Fergus," he said, "Make us a basket and bring a couple of glasses of wine while we wait."

"Is good," Ferguson laughed.

Jasper turned from Ferguson back to Frances, "You stay here, nice girl, I'll be right back," and stepped half backwards into the street.

"What are we doing?" Frances asked after him as he turned.

"I'm going to take you where you should have gone in the first place," he said over his shoulder. "But, first I have to steal a car."

The last sun tip was over, pulling all the long shadows away with it into the water. They had walked up the hills above the sea, their own shadows gliding and sliding ahead of them. Now they stood near the top, looking out, and there, at their feet, strings of stars appeared in the frail blue water, with trails of moving silver chasing them like ribbons. First one, then more and more.

"It's the fishing fleet," he said softly.

And as she watched the boats, the real stars dotted into the sky above her, point bright, one and one. Each light dipping its finger in the shivering water. And slowly in the accumulating darkness, there was no horizon, no sea, no earth. and she was standing in the sky, surrounded by the heavens.

"Listen," he said.

And there was music, carried faint along the warm evening breeze.

"It's from the radios on the boats. They're bringing you tomorrow's dinner. Let me show you something."

She didn't move.

"There," he said and turned her shoulders.

Down by the bay, lit by floodlights, the Roman ruins stood like great candles in the collecting night. And as the solid white lights traveled up the hill, she could clearly see the ancient city, where it had stood. It was real, like endless time, alive in front of her. And she could just see him, dark outline and close to her -- close enough, if she fell, tumbled into time and the sky -- he could catch her.

"That's where your friends are going to be," he said, motioning to a glowing row of gauze colored tents, stuck in the tumbled columns. And as if on cue, a set of huge headlights flashed out and cut lines high into the darkness. The faint music from the boats swallowed whole by the diesel motors of the approaching bus.

"Oh," she said and turned away.

As the noises died, he found a place in the clear night overlooking the bay. Two broken shoulders of stone, smooth with time and picnics and half lit by the far-off nearest floodlights. He spread the blanket and knelt over the basket.

"Bread, cheese, wine, olives and what i-i-s-s-s probably fish. Not quite a drunken Bulgarian Luau, but we'll get by."

"What is this?" she asked, actually speaking directly for the first time since the night had come over them.

"Hmm, Ferguson's idea of a picnic, I think."

"No, not the food. This. Is this like -- uh -- something?"

He couldn't see her face clearly, but her voice was urgent and her hands, white, were moving between them in the light. She leaned forward.

"There isn't like something going on, is there? You wouldn't do that to me?" she was shaking her head.

He understood, thought and decided.

"No," he said completely. She slipped back into the half-light.

The night was warm, like a shawl across her shoulders. She could feel it tucked into her. The music flickered, there and gone and again, melody low, recognizable pop tunes in unrecognizable languages, aroma sounds carried on the air. She could taste the night on the glistening olives, black and invisible, and on the sharp cheese that he handed her directly from the knife. And she heard his voice without the words, dark and full, deep like the wine. Its whole taste on her tongue, blending with her, blending with the night, spreading through her with no before or after, like conscious sleep.

"Sometimes," he said, "I come up here at night and just wait."

"For what? Wait for what?"

"The moon," he said.

"Is there a moon?"

"There's always a moon, Frances."

"You know what I mean. Here...now?"

"No, not tonight," he said quietly. "No sense waiting for it."

They sat for a moment, and she tucked her feet underneath her.

"What are you waiting for, then?" she said.

"Don't know. How about you?"

"I don't know. I don't think I'm really waiting for anything. Everything that's going to happen to me is just going to happen. It's not like I want very much -- a nice house, garden, children, someplace to do some good for people. What everybody else wants, I suppose."

She'd misunderstood the question, but he didn't care because she was going to tell him what she wanted to tell him -- either way.

"Okay, then, what do you want *now*?"

She shook her head in the darkness, unaware that he could barely see her.

"I don't know. I like the law. I like research. I like what I'm doing. But it's just..." She weighed her words, "I'm going to miss all kinds of things just because I don't know what they are."

She stuck her glass into the light between them, and he splashed more wine into it.

"People like me -- women like me, don't have very much – okay. We look good, not just good like attractive, our *lives* look good, and they are. But nobody ever thinks about *us*." She laughed sadly, "We're the ones who get missed. Overlooked. It's like our whole lives are clean and correct and nobody ever gives us a second thought. You know what I mean?"

He did, but he wasn't about to tell her she was doomed, and that was okay, too, because she didn't wait for him to answer.

"I'm going to be a good lawyer. I'm going to be a good mom, wife, everything -- whatever – a good -- a good person. And I'm willing to do that -- all that stuff. I just don't want to end up with nothing."

There were noises coming from below them, hard sounds that were stirring up the evening down there. She felt them, felt annoyed by them, rushed by them.

"Just – just because I'm ordinary doesn't mean I can't have something more. I look around and I see my life and I know how it's gonna go. I can see it. I'm gonna settle in and it's gonna be so-o-o easy to simply ... I don't know. Career, children, grandchildren even, houses, cars -- all that stuff -- probably end up saving the whales or feeding the orphans or something like that, and sometimes I'll even be able to convince myself that it's all good enough. But I'm gonna know it isn't -- secretly, I'm gonna know, and one day -- one day -- I'm gonna wake up and it's gonna be too late."

She paused, but there was no silence. The music and the people noise from below was more now, larger, lapping up the slopes like rising water, impossible to ignore.

"The thing is – the thing is – I don't even know what I'm looking for."

She stopped again to swallow.

"But I'm missing it. And now..."

She took a drink.

"Now. Here's this perfect night – we're having this perfect night. I've never had anything like this." her voice trailed off so she could look into the darkness. "This is the most romantic thing that's ever going to happen to me."

He moved slightly so he could see her in the light. She wasn't looking at him, so he couldn't really see her face. But she saw him move and turned her head. The light caught her eyes and they were shining in the dark, glistening with emotion. She parted her lips and swallowed, aware of him. Then, she lifted the wine glass and took a long drink.

"God! I don't know where all that came from. You must think I'm just this total poor little rich bitch. Way too much drama. I'm not like that. I'm really not. It's just the wine and...I didn't mean to..."

"Don't even think about saying you're sorry."

She laughed and sniffed and turned her face away from him.

"We're going to have to go soon, aren't we?" She said, waving vaguely at the night.

"Not really. It depends on how sick you want to be when the horde gets back to the hotel."

"I don't really care," she said, leaning back.

But she was quiet after that. Embarrassed. Aware that the mood was crumbling under the persistent pulsing music and the vague voices and scattered shrills of sound that crawled in the air around them. They sat together for awhile, feeling it die, and when it was impossible to deny that the night was gone, they left.

When he let her out of the car at the hotel, she stood with the door open and leaned inside so the brilliant lobby lights shone across her face, touching her features, shadow dark, and shaping her eyes big and bright.

"Tomorrow?"

He didn't really know. It was all turning into some kind of raggy Rom/Com tragedy, and he couldn't seem to stop it. So he just nodded and drove away.

The next morning wasn't really the next morning; it was simply something that came after the night before. The coffeepot was half empty when he got there, and she hadn't changed her clothes.

"You okay?" he said.

"Hm-um."

"Fight with the boyfriend?"

"No such luck. They were all pretty drunk when they got back last night so I just left."

"Have you been out all night?"

"I guess so. The security people woke me up this morning."

He shook his head.

"I need to get out of here," she half laughed, "Can you take me back to Europe for awhile?"

"What about your friends? Tony?"

"What about them?"

"You can't be sick forever."

"Why not?"

He looked directly at her.

"Female complications," she said, dismissing it. "He won't ask."

"Ah, yes. But can he count?"

"Don't. We're leaving tomorrow. This is my last day and I don't want to spend it…"

"Most of this isn't going to fly, Frances."

"I don't care. I'm fed up. I'm tired of missing things. I told you that last night. I need to have something even if it's only for one day."

"You need to get some sleep. You look like an unmade bed."

She didn't want to sleep. There was no time. She had spent the night in a beach chair, drowsy and dozing, listening to the waves, shining lines of water that swelled up over the sand and then slipped away back into the darkness. The sound like silk rhythms touching at her -- dreaming for her in the lullaby night. And it had all been okay. But now it was day, the last day. She could feel the sun, bright and relentless, hear the hotel noises that would eventually swallow her. All the complications and explanations she'd hidden in the darkness were real, and now there was no place for her to hide. But she wasn't going to hide. She'd already decided to run.

"They're going out on a boat – fishing." She made a face. "And I'm not going. That's it."

"That's it?"

"That's it."

Jasper looked out over the water. It was cool and blue and bright. For the first time in years, he didn't know what to do. He knew he should, but he didn't want to just say goodbye. He thought about taking her swimming, but there was no horizon out there, just endless water. That was too far for them to go today.

"Okay, it's going to be hot. Let's walk along the beach. It's the long way round into town, but you can jump in the water when you want to cool off; and if we go that way, we can stop whenever you get tired."

Frances touched her sunglasses down to her eyes and stood up.

"Do you want to change or anything?"
"No, let's just go."

Some hours later, they were still walking. They'd stopped once to hide under a big Heineken umbrella and have lunch, but mostly they just kept going. He asked her about her home and school and a few other things, but neither one of them was interested in Indiana or Tort Reform. So, as the conversation threads drifted, there were more and more silences until they just fell into step, quietly following their shadows that floated in front of them.

"Can we go for a drink somewhere?"

"Sure." he said, pointing up, "There's a bar on the roof up there."

The sun was already past, so they took their drinks out on the terrace. High over the sea, the wet breeze made it cool in the heat afternoon. She stretched her feet up onto the railing and looked out over the water. It twinkled at her. She rearranged her sunglasses and her drink, sliding them back across the table. It had all been so easy in the night. Now it was just awkward and incoherent. He was talking, but she didn't care. It was only the sound of his voice she was aware of. She turned the big neon straw round in the glass, jabbed at the ice and one-hand pretty, sipped at it.

"Where are you from here?" she said. "Where do you live?"

"There." He pointed. "Follow the water just a little further. See the green awning? That's Ferguson's. Where we were yesterday? Right behind it. The flat black roof. Those four big windows on the end. That's me."

It was dim inside the building, even though the double doors were open. The carpet was hotel beautiful, and the air was fresh and still, soundless like the lost echoes of a church.

"Just up the stairs."

She went ahead of him, into the unknown, easily directed, painfully close to the privacy of him. In her mind, it had been a gentle seduction, a hot afternoon, sweet wine and music, soft lazy touches, the feel of her to him. But here on the stairs that was gone. The fine poetic pages she had written so carefully in the night were being burned alive by pulp music and stiletto heels and the hard shiver that pulsed in the lines of her stomach.

"There," he said. And she stopped and half turned toward him, between him and the door. He would have to touch her, move her, do something with her. Jasper waited, aware, wary, about to say something. Then he just stepped forward and the pressure of him pushed her back into the unopened doorway. He stood over her and ran his hand along the waistband of her skirt. She reached her arms up and around him in acceptance. Under her clothes he could practically feel the tan line of her bikini bottom and the tiny hairs on the small of her back. Then, barely touching her, he moved his fingers up the hollow of her body. She leaned into him. He pushed his thumb into the tight fabric of her bra strap and squeezed the two hooks open with his index finger. It snapped free. Then very delicately and carefully -- he scratched.

"O-o-oh!"

She pushed her shoulder blades together.

"Oh, God. That's nice!"

She raised her left shoulder and rolled it forward.

"Right, ahhh, there."

He straightened up and her shoulder naturally followed, looking for his fingers. Then he took one slow step back, away from her arms, and his hand trailed out from underneath her clothes. They stood there, inches apart.

"What are you doing?"

"Nothing," he said slowly, shaking his head.

"It's okay."

He didn't move.

"Really, I want this. God, you don't know how much I want this."

Again he didn't move.

"What? What's the matter?"

He took a step back and half sat on the open banister.

"Do you have any idea why I was hanging around the hotel the morning we met?" he said.

"I don't care. What difference does it make? This is here. Now. What you do – Jesus -- just – Ah, shit!"

She leaned her back into the doorway.

"Don't you wonder?"

"You can't do this," she said, warning and pleading.

"You're not listening."

"What the hell are you talking about? I don't know! I don't care!"

He put both hands on the banister behind him to steady himself.

"Yes, okay. I know why you're here. I know about the music, the pressure, the drugs, the whole thing. Tony told me all about it – everything."

"Yeah, I know. I heard him. Interesting, who's calling who brain-dead."

It felt like someone was letting the air out of her legs, and she sank down the doorway and sat heavily on the floor.

"Is that what this is all about? Some stupid thing Tony said?"

He looked down at her, frustrated with the bewildered look on her face.

"For fuck sake, Frances! What do I have to do? Hit you over the head? I go to the hotel when I get bored."

There was no way around it now.

"Every summer, this place is loaded with half-naked women, okay? Sweet little middle class muffins, bored outta their minds. And they're falling all over each other, looking for an adventure. What do you think happens when they recognize a badass guitar player with my reputation?"

Jasper hesitated.

"A little wine, a little dine," he hesitated again, looking away, "A little moonlight...suddenly it's 'Girls Gone Wild,' the home game and, for three or four days, it's great dope, outrageous sex and anything else that happens to come around. Then they fly away home. Kiss, kiss, hug, hug, bye-bye. Jesus!"

He turned back and stared directly down at her.

"And just so there's no misunderstanding, when they don't recognize me, your buddy, our waiter, makes sure they do. Anything else you want to know?"

There was silence.

"Women like me." she said.

"Actually, a little older," he answered, hating himself.

She looked into the empty air for a few seconds then reached around and did up her bra strap, a little too embarrassed to adjust it in front. She stood up, took a few steps past him to the top of the stairs and turned around.

"I feel like a total idiot right now, and I really don't want to talk about this – any of this -- but you need to know something. I'm not stupid. I know what I'm doing. And I did when I came up here."

"I'll take you back to the hotel."

"That's the last place I want to be. No. I'm going across the street and have a drink or seven, and if you were any kind of a friend, you'd forget about all this," she waved her hand back into the hall, "and come with me."

"If that's what you want."

She looked into his face. Her eyes were hurt and angry, and then she turned away and walked down the stairs.

He pushed away from the banister and walked after her.

The next morning was the promise they had made to each other the night before 'just to say good-bye.' It was all tentative. There was no time left to say anything else anyway, and besides, they were both tired, tight-shouldered and weary.

"I hate to say it, but you finally look like you're actually sick," he said, half laughing.

"It's that wicked crap we ended up drinking last night."

"Local brew."

She shut her eyes and put her hand to her head.

"Oh, God."

"It's okay. We had fun."

She remembered the music and the laughter and the old women pulling her up to dance, and Yannick, Ferguson's son, swinging her into the night. She laughed.

"Yes, we did."

And she remembered at the end, Jasper holding a guitar like a lover, making it swoon and weep and Ferguson's clear voice soft as the darkness, intimate as a whisper of words she didn't understand.

"Did I say thank you?"

"Several times, and to several people."

She looked down and then up again.

"Thank you."

They sat for a moment or two, unspoken.

"I'm going to have to go before they all come down," she said finally.

"I know." And he did. He'd seen this before. She was guarding her reality, the real one. It was time to straighten up, make promises and lies and get on with it. It all mattered now. What shoes to wear? What bag to carry? Schedules and times? He thought he should explain, give her reasons, show her why, but he had no feeling for it, and she was already standing up. She pulled her bag up to her shoulder and dropped her sunglasses down over her eyes. She leaned down and kissed him slightly on the cheek, and before he could react she turned and walked away. He watched her for a few very long seconds then he stood up.

"Hey," he said loud enough for her to hear, but her footsteps didn't hesitate. "Good-bye."

The light was bold, bright in the trees. It blued the sky and cast deep shadows on the warm stones of the garden. Somewhere from the south, a lost wind gave its last exhale. It rustled the leaves, and exhausted, fell away from the heat. He could feel it -- heavy -- the long linger of summer, but yet there was something -- a faint sniff in the air, that mentioned autumn.

"I used to be better than this," he thought, and closed the book.

In all the movement and noise of the hotel morning, he wasn't actually aware of the shadow that touched the edge of his vision until it moved over him and he looked up.

"Sorry I'm late," she said and sat down beside him. "I thought I'd missed you."

"Where did you come from?"

"London. Well, not directly. Frankfurt, I think, I'm not sure. Germany, anyway."

"Really."

"Really!"

"Why did you go to Germany?"

She looked directly at him and relaxed back in her chair.

"It's a huge long story, Jasper, and I haven't slept properly for a week. Can I explain it all to you later?"

"Sure, but...." He didn't actually have anything to say so he just stopped talking.

She gave a long exhale and dropped her bag beside her.

"The thing is I started crying in London and I just couldn't stop."

Jasper turned a cup over for her and filled it with coffee.

"I didn't know what to do, so I just walked away."

"You walked from London?"

"It probably would have been faster."

She sipped her coffee.

"So, what now?" Jasper asked, genuinely interested.

"I don't know. I haven't got any money. A few hundred dollars. If you won't take me in, I don't have a place to stay, and the parents are probably going to disown me when they find out I'm not going back to school."

"You're not going back to school?"

"Don't get all uncomfortable -- just not right now. You haven't ruined my life, jus-s-st this part of it. Look, I don't really know what I'm going to do. This is all new to me. But I had to come back and find out what we started here."

"We?"

"We, Jasper," she said definitively.

"Are you sure about this?"

"No, not really, but I'm not going to miss this. Not this time. I almost did, and I thought I was gonna die."

"Okay," he said, "But you know I have to leave this all up to you."

She looked out at the ocean and the sky and then back into Jasper's face.

"I know. But right now I'm deadly tired and we've got all the time in the world to figure out the wherefores and the whys. I'm going to finish my coffee and then you're going to take me home and put me to bed."

Seventeen days later, she sat on the edge of the patio in the restaurant across the street from the apartment. Jasper was sleeping or something, and she was tired and hungry. It was barely evening in that quiet time before dark but long after it was afternoon. There were a few groups of early old tourists having drinks before dinner. Scattered around the restaurant, they looked like big pastel candies left over from an Easter egg hunt. She felt scuffed and puffy, and it might have been Thursday but she wasn't sure. She ran her thumbnail down the groove in the wooden table pushing a crumbly curl of dirt ahead of it. She brushed it away with her hand and reached for one of the black cigarettes that Jasper occasionally smoked. This was going on and on, each ending simply leading to the next thing. There was no time, no morning, no night, no reflective bit of pause, just each thing stumbling into the next one. But the wine was cold, and she could smell a pot of mussels boiling in the kitchen. Besides, if there was an end to it, it wasn't here.

"Lady, what you want?"

It was the big familiar voice from the kitchen. She laughed and the Easter eggs stopped to listen. She held her hands out high in the air to indicate a bowl.

"Big one?" the voice filled the room and ran into the street.

She shook her head and shrank her hands together.

"Ah, 's good."

She brought her hands down, the Easter eggs went back to their own conversations, and she went back to her wine and cigarette. She looked across the street, up into the four unlit windows. She could see the inarticulate darkness settling into them, turning their long shadows into mirrored night. The nights were huge here, like everything else, all the empty spaces filled with touch and sight and feeling. But just as big as everything seemed to be, she knew, for her, there were no infinites. She hadn't lost the law; she'd misplaced it -- along with her deodorant, mascara and razor. The evil taste in her mouth was transient debauchery dry, and even the black blonde thumbprint bruises on her arm weren't scars and never would be. She leaned back and stretched her head onto her shoulder, and, like sleepy, winced her eyes. Once, in the light shadowed balcony that overlooked the street beside her, she'd asked him why. The one big, one word, half-naked, 3 o'clock in the morning, question.

"At some point," he said, "When everything was going to hell the first time, I realized I wasn't going to die young. People – strangers," he half laughed, "were going to watch me get old and scabby. I was going to end up a facelift or a fossil … grubbing around on my reputation. It was embarrassing."

She had meant, "Why me?" But she didn't stop him.

"The problem was – is -- I *like* it. I still do. I miss it. But when I tried it again," he took a hissing breath between his teeth, "it just – just -- I realized I was on the edge of old and it wasn't going to work, so I left -- wandered around for awhile and ended up here. And now it's perfect. I'm not old, anymore. Nobody knows what I used to be – sometimes the tourists do, but that's a plus and it's temporary." He moved his shoulders. "I'm rich. I can do what I want. Nobody bothers me. I can work when I want," he shrugged again, "play when I want, sing, write. And I've got tons of opportunities to indulge myself." He motioned his hand over the curve of her belly. "Sex, drugs and rock 'n roll. What more do I need? And nobody's watching. To everybody – everything – even now," he turned his face to her, "I'm the perfect memory."

And she knew it; she saw it. Life's one compelling purpose -- to shimmer under the lights. To ultimately mean something to somebody. And she was part of that. Like all the others, she would remember, long after her grandchildren were grown and married, she would remember. On cold dark nights that were lonely and old, she would have him, just like this, and the secret warm feeling that for one shining moment, she was the center of all the world. And she loved him for that and touched his hand to her stomach, holding, and knowing why she was the perfect audience who would never get tired of the show.

She shook her head, the hair out of her face and stretched her neck. But that question hadn't appeared somewhere in the vague measureless time of days and nights. It had happened last night; actually, that morning, and she hadn't really slept since then. The Easter eggs stopped and watched the procession of mussels steaming to her table, and she heard from above the street.

"Where've you been?"

She turned her head up to the balcony.

"I'm going to Rome," she shouted

"Home?" shouted back

"Rome!" answered louder, "I called the parents. I'm going to do it right this time."

"Brilliant. Can I come?"

The Easter eggs were interested now, and Jannick hovered.

"You're the guest of honor."

She raised her glass of wine and shook it slightly in the air. "You want some?"

"I'll be right down." He turned away from the banister and then turned back. "Does Tony know?"

"Not yet," she said and drank her wine at him.

It was still warm, but... It wasn't a chill but the feel of the air. The seam of the season, the subtle stitching that held summer to autumn, that bare touch, that was just before the leaves turned color. Somewhere from the north, a lost wind gave its last exhale. It rustled the leaves, and scattered itself away out over the garden. He could smell it, taste it. The last linger of what had been summer. Like something fading out of his memory. That's better, he thought, and he looked out toward the hotel. The long lines of tables were shorter, the tourists weren't so many and not so well-dressed, and the tablecloths were gone. He sat with his back to the water, not even concentrating, just tracking the middle distance from his mind to the hotel in the space between thought and word, half seeing without knowing it.

"Excuse me." The voice was clearly female. "I'm sorry to bother you, but ... uh ... this sounds crazy..."

He looked up at the woman and beyond her to the friend who sat, expectantly casual, at a table just out of his direct vision. He knew the type: a few years older than they looked, but definitely younger than their manner suggested. He had seen them come down together and generally take possession of their space, big hats, bags on extra chairs, and much activity for the waiter.

"I know you? I mean, I think I know you -- uh -- you look so familiar. I and my friend," she gave a wave back without looking, "we've been trying to place you. There something...you look like... Are you Jasper Conrad?"

"I don't think so," he said, smiling up at her.

The answer stunned her, and she moved her head back.

"Oh!" she said.

"Not to worry. I get that a lot. Apparently, we look alike but, he's not quite as handsome as I am."

The woman laughed.

"Oh, I am sorry but the resemblance is amazing. You could be brothers. My name's Teri, by the way. My friend and I," she waved her hand vaguely again, "We arrived last night. We're here for a week. Get away from it all and all that. Are you?" she pointed to the ground and kept speaking before he could answer.

"Maybe later we could buy you a drink to make up for interrupting your breakfast?"

"That's awfully nice of you," he said kindly. "I'm flattered, but no, actually, I'm waiting for someone."

------/\------

....A Simple Thing

On a chilly, grey December morning, Lester B. Taylor readjusted his life and decided to go home. That's not strictly true. What he decided was he couldn't go back to the apartment; home was just the logical alternative. And if he had to go home, he had to re-become what he was, or at least what he had been, before Paris. He couldn't very well show up like this. Most everything else was just cold and godawful in the light of day. So he just sat there with his coffee and cigarettes like a hideous hangover that occasionally winces its regrets.

Lester B. Taylor had come to Paris six months earlier on a glorious June afternoon reeking with sunshine. He'd stopped at St-Michel and carried his suitcases up the hill to the Sorbonne, sat down with a deep red glass of Bordeaux and knew he could conquer the world. His world anyway. Then he went off to find Jack, a friend from the old days who'd offered him bed and breakfast, cheap and convenient.

The plan was simple. He had been deemed excellent enough by his colleagues to get a year's paid leave from the college to write a book. And not just any book, *the* book: the one that had been rolling around inside him ever since graduate school. The one that would separate him from the historian horde and recreate Lester B. Taylor as the young and brilliant go-to guy of the French Revolution. He had spent most of the spring worrying librarians over obscure volumes, cleaning out the garage, dueling with the Internet, and retiling the bathroom. Then, as they agreed, the summer and fall semester would be direct research in Paris. Maridee and the kids would join him for Christmas and they'd all go home together.

So simple. Come to Paris, read, study and create the last, all-knowing final word on Danton's Vision in the French Revolution, 1789 - 1794 (his rewritten thesis, actually). Then go home, accept the accolades, become the youngest chairman of his department and a future authority in the field and then...and then. He hadn't really thought much beyond that.

But Paris had been excited to see him again anyway, all pencil-sharp bright in the long warm summer, full of wonderful people and happy cafes. He settled in. He negotiated his research card in stumbling, smiling French. He phoned home. Most days he went to the university early and ate his lunch in the Jardin du Luxembourg. He found his "Passe Historique" French wasn't as good as he thought and the reading was slow -- but steady, despite the difficulties. He phoned home again and talked to the kids. Some days, in the brilliant afternoons, he'd abandon the library and wander, getting the feel of the place and visiting with history. He rediscovered Monet and Degas. He took a day and went to Versailles. He found a little café on Rue Danton and another one on Petit Pont. He found his stilted academic French wasn't quite so cute when people were busy. He phoned home again and interrupted Maridee fighting with the furnace man and Jessica going out with her friends. The Metro wasn't so crowded mid morning, so he could sleep late. He found Shakespeare's and Abbey Books. Good friends aren't necessarily good landlords. He discovered another café facing the river that played jazz late into the evening. He reread his thesis. He lounged. Dull-eyed paintings and dry pen oratory. He drank wine. He watched women. Maridee and the kids were busy. He lost interest. A couple of long-winded mystery novels. Jack was an asshole. A confrontation. He started looking for an apartment. Then he met her.

"God, just give it the cheap melodrama," he thought.

He knew her. He had seen her before. It wasn't a flash from the sky, voltage from the blue. They hadn't spoken, but... you don't hang around the neighborhood cafes in Paris without recognizing the locals who frequent them. She had been there. So it wasn't a total stranger who stood over his table that evening. He had asked around about apartments, and although most people had just shrugged and maybe-d, Gaston had mentioned that

Madame Estain may know of something. Madame, up close and personal, looked about 18 years old.

"Hello. You are the American man who is looking for an apartment?"

"Close enough," he said. "Do you know of one around here? Not too expensive; I'm on a bit of a budget."

They stared at each other awkwardly for a moment.

"Ehm, sorry. Excuse my manners. Would you care to sit down?" he said, indicating the chair across the table without getting up.

"Thank you," she nodded and awkwardly pulled the chair out for herself.

"I'm Les, Les Taylor." he said, holding out his hand, "And you are?"

The was a hesitation while she sat down.

"Yes, of course," she said, "My name is Julianne Estain," and she shook his hand. "I've have seen you here many times. Are you going to stay in Paris a long time?"

"Only about four months more, I'm afraid. I have to finish my book."

"Of course," she said, knowingly.

"I'm having a little trouble with the friend I'm staying with, and I thought it would be best if I moved out while we were still friends."

"Of course," she said again.

"There are many apartments in this area, but most of them go to rich tourists who want to stay here in the city. They like the galleries and the restaurants, Notre Dame. Many writers come to Paris also. But they are not tourists. Tourists can pay. This is the good part. But it's bad for the people."

"Yes," he agreed, but as she spoke he found himself looking beyond her into the trees, brilliant green and jeweled by the lights from the river and the cathedral. They looked like shivering emeralds. He could hear her words, soft and spoken, but, in fact, he began drifting on the sound of them. And there was -- somewhere -- music, and the far away cutlery clatter of cups and dishes and people walking in and out of the evening in the quiet there-and-gone tones of Parisian French. And she was young and close enough to touch. And the wine was deep red. He could feel it, on his fingers, through the smooth round bottom of the wine glass. And somehow it all became Paris – The Paris. The one he'd been looking for. The one he'd misplaced in the spitless dry pages of the Sorbonne. Paris with a 50s Bardot accent and long white aprons, ankle-tied fuck-me shoes and accordion music. It was alive in the voice of one of its granddaughters. He could see it in her face and all around her. Suddenly, he was talking then too, expressive with wine, explaining, and she listened to him. He told her about his problems with Jack, and the research, and the book itself. And as he spoke, he watched her follow his voice, actually listening, sympathizing with his difficulties, her face half-light bright against the darker night of Paris that was living behind her. It reignited his waned enthusiasm. And they talked together. Laughing in the right spots, listening, speaking, telling him ordinary things, hearing his complications. She knew what Paris was, and she showed it to him. She told him about Gaston the waiter, Ardele and Yousef, and the gruff fellow Mearse they all called Monsieur Le Merde and she mimicked his Breton accent just as if he could hear the difference, and he pretended he did. She was beautiful, pooled in the light of their table. Their table? The table. When it was time, she simply touched his arm to indicate more wine and big pieces of bread with cheeses and fruit.

"We will have a bargain, you and I." She said, "You need the time and a place. I have these things; I can give them to you."

And none of it was real, but it all seemed so reasonable. And he didn't understand any of it, but he thought he did. And he agreed anyway.

She knew of an apartment, very near, in the building where she lived. It was just around the corner, and she had the key.

On a chilly December morning, it seemed so much more seductive than it really was, the way he remembered it all, not clearly, but... He was sitting at the same table. The one they sat at nearly every morning. No, he couldn't go back to the apartment. He thought he had somewhere else to go, so he stood up and went. She would cover the bill, she always had -- but -- then he didn't think so – maybe? But they were his friends too, so he went back. But he didn't wave or say goodbye; he just left money on the table and walked away. On St-Michel, he deliberately stopped and looked into the face of the Sorbonne, so he could say goodbye. Just as if things were ordinary, and nothing had happened and he was just going home. Then he kept walking – up -- away from the river. To where? He didn't know – home? But everything he had was still in the apartment. He didn't have any clothes or even very much money. He hadn't thought of it. He hadn't actually thought of anything. He needed time to think of things, stop dead, halt everything and make some real choices. So he did. But standing in the promise of another Paris day, all he could do was shiver at the thought of actually thinking "real choices." What the hell did that even mean? And sagging into the building behind him, he tried not to cry.

That night, she had taken him there: just around the corner, up the three short flights of stairs and through the green door on the right. She showed him where the towels were, turned on the hot water, stood on tiptoes and kissed him on both cheeks. Then she put the key on the table, said "Bonne nuit" and walked away, closing the door behind her and leaving him standing there.
"See if you like it," she had said. "Tomorrow we can decide. It's very late. Le Métro is finished anyway. C'est bon."
That was it. That was how he came to live in the little apartment at the top of the stairs, the one directly across from hers. No debate, no discussion. They just did it. C'est bon.

The next morning he woke up easily, feeling a little hungover and a lot foolish. And even though he'd half talked himself out of it, she wasn't convinced when he met her again, at the same table they had sat at the night before.

"Les, listen to me. Remember we have made a bargain. I am a woman by myself, alone. Sometimes some people think this is a reason to take advantage. I need some man to be there -- available, visible -- so sometimes people think another thing. So, I need this thing. So, you need a place to live, to work, to write your book. Boom! Fini!"

She gestured, with her hands open.

"This is my building. I am your landlord. You live there, work, do what you want. At night, when I come home, I will ring your bell. You come out and say to me, 'Hello Julianne. How are you, Julianne? Did you have a nice day?' That's all."

She folded her newspaper, and set it down beside her.

"It's a simple thing."

It seemed so simple at the time and so insane, sagged alone against a stone-chilled wall. What the hell was he thinking? He needed to think. He straightened himself and went around the corner and sat down at another available table and lit a cigarette.

"I'll have to quit smoking again," he thought. But what he said was, "Bonjour. Café, si vous plaît."

Down by the river, the bells of Notre Dame rose through the chilly air and woke her. She padded naked from the bedroom across the cool floor to the bathroom. She looked in the mirror intently and ran her tongue gingerly around the inside of her mouth. Then she went back through the big room to the kitchen, shook the kettle, and turned on the stove. She grabbed a sheet off the bed and wrapped it around her. Then she pulled open the curtains and sat down in the window. She lit a cigarette and blew the smoke high out, so it billowed against the ceiling. She could see his windows directly across the courtyard from where she was sitting.

It didn't take him very many evenings to figure out what was going on. The first man was a friend, but then there were more. And, every time, she would ring his bell and he would touch the button to let her in, then go out and stand dutifully by his door and watch them come up the stairs.
"Bonsoir, Julianne."
"Bonsoir."
Somewhere in the week, he realized it was a business – a business full of men and women in various combinations. It was awkward then, because, from the very first, they had taken their mornings together at the little café by the river. And after a few more mornings and a few more nights, it became uncomfortable, so he simply didn't mention it.

Julianne Estain was an articulate and knowledgeable young woman. She liked hot chocolate, buttery croissants, ice cream and Marlboros. She spoke several languages. It was none of his business. She read *Le Figaro* and didn't like to brush her hair, keeping it back from her face with a couple of quick fingering combs. She was interested in what he did. She asked questions, offered comment and advice. He began to work again and had things to tell her. He liked their mornings, late and leisured, with hand-hot cups wisping steam into the crisp air. Her chin cuddled down into a big knot sweater or hidden in a scarf. The way she laughed or scowled or explained the political cartoons. It really was none of his business. She was young and fun, and he saw them together that way, fresher than the people he knew, and really not much younger. At night, with her hair up, painted, posed and dressed in the hard-cut severe fashions she favored, she looked her age. His age? No, but close enough.

The sun, burning through a thinner patch of cloud, reflected its bright oval face in the window and disappeared. She pulled the sheet around her, toga style, and got up and walked across the landing to his door. She didn't hesitate but knocked loud and boldly, as she had done for the last few months. When there was no answer she went back and pulled on jeans and a sweater, turned the heat off the half-boiled water, finger-combed her hair on the way out, and went down to get a real coffee.

He was some few streets away, just sitting, the city moving around him, waking and stretching and going to work. He wasn't thinking. He couldn't think. He didn't have any choice, real or otherwise. He felt like he hadn't slept for weeks. He could see the house and the yard and the broken pole by the gate. His house? His yard? He remembered the long hall at the college, but it was empty and clean. The students, faceless and silent. All the people he used to know crumbling and old, worn dry with global concerns and relentless entertainment. The taste of hamburgers, the feel of driving, the noise of television -- all the things that made him what he had been -- were gone. All he knew for certain was he was sitting alone on the verge of another Paris day. Lester B. Taylor in a free fall failed semester? Monsieur La Clef in a dangerous black Versace suit? He could remember Maridee's face when they made love, but he couldn't hear the sounds she made. He could still hear, however, quite clearly, the sounds of Julianne, face down on the bed, her peach-flavored fingernails digging into the pillow. But it wasn't like that. He couldn't explain it to her -- either her -- or to anybody.

"Believe me, I don't know what happened or how, and I sure as hell don't know why, but..." Jesus H. Christ! What was he going to do?

The afternoon he asked her "Why?" she was scrubbing the outside of their building where someone had scrawled several black graffiti symbols.

"Look at this," she shouted, swinging her brush wildly. "These pigs come and piss all over my house! Look at it!"

He set his books down on the street, and reached for the brush.

"Pigs!" she shouted into the busy street, "I will piss on you!"

"Here, let me do that."

She recoiled from him, moving the brush defensively behind her.

"No," she said anxiously, "You can't do this."

"Why not? I'm good at it. Believe me, I've had tons of practice back home."

"That is there and this is here," she said, holding her ground. "Here, you are not a workman."

"Neither are you," he said.

She looked at him deeply for a couple of seconds, and then she laughed, and all the anxiety and anger melted away.

"You are very correct," she said, "I was made for better things. Come now, no more work."

She tucked the bucket inside the door and brought out her purse and a trim jacket.

"Today we will have fun. Only mad dogs and horses work all day."

"Fools and horses," he corrected. "Mad dogs and Englishmen."

She looked at him.

"First we will have lunch and shopping and tonight I will take you to my club."

"You own a club?"

"No, no, no. It's where I work."

"Oh, I – uh – have some more work, to do." He shook his head and bent down to pick up his books, "I'm kind of busy with – uh – some things -- and…"

She reached down and touched him on the arm.

"Les," she said, deliberately making him pause, "Some days in the month I don't work."

"Oh, yes," he muttered awkwardly, "Of course."

They started down the street.

"You want to know why. Everyone wants to know why."

"No, really I'm…" he answered even though it was exactly what he was thinking.

"Let me tell you some things," she said, walking along.

"When I was in the university I studied what you call -- uh -- Les Commerces -- uh -- Business. I went to work at a bank, Credit Lyonnais, making business plans, models for development. I was paid well, and if I worked hard, I could live well. Pretty good, but I also knew another thing. The customers I was making the models for were getting rich -- very rich. I want to be rich also, of course, so I took some time and made another model -- a plan for me. It was difficult but I knew it was a good plan. So.... Now I own a building and people pay me rent. I invest. I have a café. Sometime, maybe, with some luck, I will be rich. Rich people don't have to work. They can do what they like."

They paused to assess the traffic.

"But if you have all these things, why do you still -- uh -- work?"

She smiled.

"So I can go shopping and buy you some decent clothes," she said laughing, pulling at his sweater. They made a dash across the street. On the other side, she stopped and looked at him seriously.

"It's a simple thing. To get rich, you need assets. But you have to work also."

She slid her hands down her body from her breasts into a V at the bottom of her belly.

"I have assets," she said, looking straight at him, "That have no expense and don't pay taxes. But... not forever. Right now, today, you see, I am a young woman but... five years, maybe ten... no."

She touched her face.

"I get... hmmm...wrinkles, the bird's feet, some more chins and a fat bum from le chocolat?" she shrugged, "My assets will be gone. So, I must work very hard while I can. That was the plan I made. You see. But this is the story for you." she said, "Between us."

She started walking again.

"If I don't work now, no money. No money? No house, no food, no nothing. No place to write your book." she said over her shoulder.

"I understand," he said, catching up to her, "I don't ju – I mean -- I'm not judgmental. But why me? Wha... What...?"

"You are insurance," she said, stopping again against the flow of pedestrians and turning to face him.

"I am a small woman, surrounded by big men. I can tell them what are the rules, but I can't make them. If they are rough, I have problems. Maybe they can hurt me," she shook her head. "No. You are insurance."

"But why me? Why not somebody here? I'm..."

"People here are very complicated. They want to know what you do and then they try to tell you what to do, and maybe they need money. Ahhh. No. You and I," she shook her index finger back and forth between them, "Between you and I it's a simple thing."

"But I'm not a... I'm a history professor."

"They don't know that," she said slyly and starting walking again.

And they didn't. And after that very first night at Le Club, they even convinced him. He wasn't really Lester B. Taylor; he was Monsieur La Clef or La Clef Anglaise. He was with Julianne Estain, or, more importantly, she was with him.

Le Club itself wasn't even a club; it was just a big expensive party that never stopped. Just one street off Rue Galande. It was a huge catacomb underneath a regular restaurant called Barney's. But if you didn't know it was there, you'd never find it, and if you did stumble on it, by accident, they wouldn't let you in. It was members only, and everyone knew someone, but no one knew everybody. A timeless twilight world without night or light, continuously feeding on varying degrees of intimacy.

It was one long room, with low medieval arches on rows of grey pillars that cast deep corners into the stone and made dark crevices. There was a stage at the far end that fought for the uncertain light. People crowded there to writhe with the music or stand close to the show, but others sat away in the flickering darkness. These were the shadows -- attended by men, totally covered in half-naked silk -- they drank wine from hard crystal glasses, smoked black African drugs from ornate hookahs and ate with their fingers from heavy silver trays. They had no real voices, just low sounds that dissolved into the air; no clear faces, just features that moved in and out of the dim. They emerged and descended like dancing dark flames, licking at the walls. They spoke and giggled and whispered -- but they never touched each other. It was forbidden. Deprived of light and denied their touch, some moved through the crowd like predators, sniffing. Some huddled together murmuring their secrets at intimate distance. Some perched alone like birds of prey, some like the prey they were seeking. And some settled and rose and settled again, agitated beyond their ability to be still. The music came and ceased and came again in an endless rhythm of dark exotic dances, pagan rites and breathing erotic performances. In the eternal twilight of Le Club, it was a smooth throb that never slept.

"Stay with me," Julianne had said the first time, and soon they were in a group by the wall, talking and watching. Several times, people came by and placed their mouths next to her ear. Each time, she smiled and gestured in front of him, with her open palm like she was holding his face in her hand. And even though he couldn't see them clearly, he could feel them there, near her, coiled and taut. Each new tension on top of the one before, held onto them and over them by the low ceiling and the music and the hard lights glistening on the sweat-stained stage. It was real. He could feel it. It wasn't a strange footstep on the stairs, an unknown face or a nodded "bonsoir." It was need, want, the ache in the low of the belly. No flame of passion, just a hard steady hurt. Desire growling in the darkness.

"It was so simple after that," he thought, lightly tossing his cigarette into the street. He was never quite Lester B. Taylor again. He could fake it, over the phone or in emails but... The things that were him; the shell of him, collected and cultivated over the years, just dried up, cracked off and blew away, with the autumn leaves of Paris. His friends and colleagues -- bearded or bagged in long brown dresses, academic fundamentalists, all earnest and petty and jealous -- just disappeared. His students, black-minded little bastards, afraid of themselves and striving -- gone. And his own life, chained to a thousand-year mortgage to pay for years of two careers, two cars, two children and two of just about everything else -- vanished. So he just stopped. He took up smoking again and drank wine and laughed at the tourists and gossiped with the waiters. He spent his days researching and writing his book, making it better than it was ever going to be, his nights waiting on a delicious French whore, and his mornings full of coffee and conversation with Julianne, in the little café by the river.

At the café she pushed the cup and saucer away and tapped the neatly-stacked Euros with her finger.
"Yousef," she said, "Oú est Monsieur?"
Yousef, who was from a canny village on the road to Oran, shrugged and turned away. She slapped the table with her fingers in a quiet but unmistakable way.
"Oú est Monsieur?" she said again, sharply.
Yousef pointed up the street and stood dumb, waiting.
She didn't move her eyes.
"Cinq ou dix minutes, chérie," he said finally.

He didn't know who started the shouting and clapping the night Julianne danced at Le Club. He heard a single voice first then another and more and more hands together rising over the heads of a Lucifer and his demons who lay sprawled across the stage, streaked with sweat and make-up.
"Julianne!" they shouted.
And then it was "Julianne!" from there and there.
"Julianne!"
"Julianne!" Clapping and stomping.
"Julianne! Julianne!" urgent and persistent, until she stood up, smoothed her grey skirt over her hips and stepped up to the stage. There was cheering and applause and then a gathering silence until only the sound of her heels on the steps

echoed in the room. She looked around at the demons on the floor as though she'd never seen them before, questioning, stepping between them and among them. And then there was music, slow and low. It swayed over her and she moved with it, reaching her hands, slowly dancing the demons up to her, conjuring them back to life. And they crawled to her, grasping and standing, their chests wide and their bellies hollow with hunger. And the music began beating down into them, contorting them forward, searching, seeking. And she glided her body around them, lilting on the gathering music that was travelling through her. Slipping over them, stroking them, coaxing them, feeling their heat touching her. And they crowded against her, their muscles tight and clinching, so close their nostrils flared with her smell. And she danced to them, a female soul, dining on desire, her body heaving with breath. And the music quickened, its hard beat pulsing like a single throbbing torso. And they all moved together in its rhythm. She matched them movement for movement, holding them to her, tightening her steps, accepting the power that was closing and closing and closing onto itself. And every person in the room saw her separately. Each one of them danced with her separately. Each one of them, feeling her separately. Holding her, helping her, craving her release. Until she held them balanced on the edge of themselves, their muscles tight and urgent. And the music thumped and thumped and thumped against them and the demons rose in the air and she flung her head back, eyes half closed, mouth panting, and suspended on one silent scream, the music howled and she collapsed on the stage. And they all gasped and could breathe again. He felt them silently watch her stand up and saw their eyes follow her back to the table where she sat down beside him, crossed her legs neatly at the ankles, reached in front of him and took a sip from his wine glass.

He remembered the lipstick taste of the glass, even the texture of it on his lips. He wondered if Maridee wore lipstick. He thought she did, at least she used to -- maybe? It was things like that that he just couldn't remember, little things that were the real memory. He saw the rest of it clearly, his whole life, but it was clean and dry and sterile. There were no footsteps, no scratching, no taste, no smell; it was almost as if he'd read it in a book.

"I'll never be able to do it," he thought. 'I've gone too far for that."

Sitting drunk on the edge of oblivion, the grey smoke hanging thick in the air of Gaston's tiny apartment. Laughing and singing and trying to negotiate the overstuffed chairs. Yousef playing the torn arm of the sofa next to his head, like a tabla drum, translating the thick guttural Arabic songs. Julianne swaying through the room.

"I have a song. I have a song," like an overeager schoolgirl.

But it was bad and she forgot the words and tumbled over an unidentified body. They whistled and hissed and threw things.

"No, no, I have a real song," she said, giggling and standing again.

"In French, but I will translate," she gestured widely to the room. "For you."

And she started singing in Arabic, some folk song that many of them knew and sang along. It steadied her and she pantomimed the parts, holding her sleeve up to her face for a veil. It seemed like a sad song to him.

"Qu'est-ce que, Yousef?"

"It's about a girl from the 'bled' in my country. She comes to Paris without her family and she is lonely. She – uh – she - uh – she has some men, but they are mean to her." Yousef stopped talking to sing the chorus. Then quickly.

"But she wants to be a good girl. Is there no one who will help her? No one who knows her heart?"

Julianne's voice changed, and most of them laughed. And then she was standing in front of him, twirling her skirt in front of his face. He turned to Yousef who was drumming again and singing the chorus.

"The men promise her beautiful earrings but only want to – uh…" Yousef searched for the words, "pierce her ears. Like men everywhere. But I want to be a good girl. Is there no one who will help me? No one with the key to my heart?"

The beat was faster and Julianne was dancing directly over him, trembling her hips so her full skirt brushed across his face. The song had turned from rhythm to rap, and she was obviously changing the words. Yousef tried to keep up, drumming and translating, but he was laughing, and he only got parts of the song. And everyone else was laughing too.

"Here is a man with the key to my heart but it – uh – he doesn't use it – uh – more – uh - much…"

The joke was becoming clear, even without translation.

"Maybe it's small – uh – a key so small it can't open -- the ga…the lock…or maybe…"

Julianne pulled her skirt up obscenely over her hips shaking the hem, offering him waving glimpses of the dark triangle of her panties -- gyrating her hips and jerking impatiently.

"Maybe it is – uh – maybe it…" Yousef waved his arm loosely in the air, laughing.

"Maybe it wiggles?" he said seriously, looking around. Julianne stopped short. With the drink and the drugs, it was all too hilarious, and the two of them collapsed together, laughing. Everyone was laughing, uncontrollably. Finally, Julianne pushed Yousef away, and with mock dignity, straightened herself, adjusted her clothes, and began the song again, in English, her accent thick with alcohol.

"Oh, Monsieur; I don't want to be a good girl! Can you help me please, oh please find the key to my heart. Because I'm really not a good girl, but I'll be good for you. If you can please oh please use the key to…"

But before she could finish, Yousef waved his arm madly in the air again, flopping it around uncontrollably and they were gone again, laughing and snorting and literally rolling on the floor.

"It wasn't that funny," he thought, looking back into the sun-broken, morning. But at least it was real. He could still feel the embarrassed sting of it. Not like that vague somewhere, where he had a home and a wife, children and a career. What was that? Some photograph-thin reality that wouldn't go away? No, actually that was reality, and no amount of wishful thinking could change that. Whether he liked it or not, he had to go home. It was what he had to do. Today. Because no matter how mundane, dredging, trudging bad-dream-bad he knew his life was, anything, absolutely anything, was preferable to walking the three streets down to the river and Julianne. He shivered.

Julianne dipped her croissant into the hot chocolate and carefully took a bite. She picked the buttery flakes off the surface with her finger and touched them to her tongue.
"Yousef?" she questioned and gestured slowly at the café with her palms open and her shoulders hunched.
"No." he replied, shaking his head dismissively. "There was some trouble. In the night -- some shouting and noise. That's all, chérie."
She nodded

"That man is a pig. Everyone knows."

"Yes," she said, lighting a cigarette, "We must find Monsieur."

"We?" he replied. " No, chére, no. It's none of my business. Between…" He motioned back and forth with his hands. "No!"

"Yousef," she asked, slouching in her chair.

They looked at each other. They were old friends, and they knew each other well.

The sun was up now, bright and crisp. He realized he didn't have a coat. He hadn't noticed before, even though he'd been out most of the night. He was no closer to doing whatever it was that he was going to do. So he lit another cigarette and sat. In the brighter light, it wasn't just chaos anymore. He wasn't Lester B. Taylor -- he knew that -- and he was never going to be that ever again. But maybe Monsieur La Clef was dead too; maybe he committed suicide somewhere, in the night. Was it only last night? Was it only yesterday? Was the only thing left sitting there a bag of mortality, waiting to get up and begin its journey to the grave? And he did cry then, long gurgling sobs that he hid with his hand on his forehead, his shoulders shaking. He was tired and cold and alone, and he knew that now, and he didn't know how to change it. He didn't want to think anymore; he just wanted to go home -- somebody's home -- and go to sleep.

"Was it really only last night?" he thought. It seemed like weeks ago he heard the scream -- not a scream actually, a shout -- more in anger than in pain. He hurried out of his apartment, crossed the landing and pushed open the door.

"Julianne?"

Julianne was sprawled, topless, on the floor, next to the bed, screaming obscenities, in two or three different languages, the side of her mouth dripping blood. The man who had come up the stairs with her earlier was standing over her, his shirt open and his trousers undone. Les stepped between them, pushed the man out of the way, and bent down to help Julianne. She looked up at him in incredible surprise. The man kicked him viciously in the ribs, and he staggered to get up, swinging wildly into the air. The man dodged him easily and backed away, bringing up his fists. Les had never actually fought with anyone in his life, but the pain and the situation turned into simple instinct, and he charged into the man, right from the floor, knocking him off balance and slamming him into the wall. He threw a couple of clumsy punches, in close, and the man struggled against him, grabbing the back of his hair. It hurt, and his head snapped back. The man pulled harder and pushed with his shoulder, trying to escape, but his trousers drooped and he staggered. Les reacted quickly and brought his knee up hard into the man's groin. He howled and went limp, letting go of his hair. Les brought his knee up again. This time with all his force, holding the man by the shoulders to get a good solid hit and nearly lifting him off his feet. The man fell forward, spitting and choking, gagging on the pain. He stepped away, and the man fell to his knees and then forward onto his face, clutching his groin, slobber and slime coming out of his nose and mouth. Les stepped back, his chest heaving. Then he kicked the man a glancing blow in the stomach, just to make sure he didn't get up. The man retched forward, moaning. Julianne was still shaking by the side of the bed, and he turned and lifted her onto her feet. Furious, she tried to dodge around him, to get at the man on the floor.

"Wait! Just wait!" he said, and grabbed her face in his hands. He dabbed the blood away with the sleeve of his shirt. There was no mark, so he pushed her lip down and saw the gash on the inside of her mouth. She struggled and....

"Stop it. Let me see! Stop it. Quit, goddamn it."

He bodily threw her down on the bed. She scrambled to get up. He pushed her back, holding her face down with the weight of his body across her shoulders. She strained against him.

"Stop it!"

"You fucking cock bastard!" she howled, incoherent with rage.

He leaned down harder, holding her tight against the bed, and, without any thought at all, reached out with his free hand and slapped the dark blue triangle of her panties with his open palm. She stopped writhing and kicked her legs out. He did it again, spanking her like a child. Spanking her because she wouldn't stop, wouldn't listen to him. Spanking her out of frustration and anger and the adrenaline of the moment and because he could. And because she wasn't an accountant, and she'd made fun of him at a party and he wasn't sure it was a joke. He spanked her because, for the first time in his adult life, he felt strong -- like a warrior -- and it was her fault. She had made him into Monsieur La Clef. And he spanked her because he liked it. And he spanked her because he'd been with her every day for months, and he liked the way she laughed, and accountants don't get hit in the mouth by some fuckin' weirdo in the middle of the night. And he spanked her because he wanted to sleep with her, and hold her, and comb the hair away from her face with his fingers. And he spanked her because everybody else did too, and he was jealous. And he spanked her because he hadn't been very good 'insurance' and she'd gotten hurt and he felt ineffectual and useless to her.

Even though it had been less than a minute -- less than thirty seconds -- it felt like hours, and he stopped. He heard the man groaning on the floor, and Julianne gasping and whimpering her face into the pillow. She was surprisingly little, lying there. He slowly eased his weight off her and she didn't move, her body clenched rigid into the bed. He moved away from her. She turned her face towards him, her eyes half-closed, her makeup tear-streaked and ruined. He stood up. There was no sound except the man on the floor and Julianne catching rapid little breaths of air. They waited, watching each other. The man on the floor moved, and he turned his head towards them. Two deliberate steps and Les had him by the hair, pulled him up and kicked him in the face. The man grunted and retched again against the blood in his mouth. Julianne growled into the bed, bouncing her head and shoulders into the pillow with frustration. Les grabbed the man under the arms and pushed him towards the door. He stumbled heavily. Julianne flung herself over onto her back and sat up on her knees. Les threw the man's coat onto the floor and swirled it around with his foot, cleaning up the mess. Julianne, her anger dissolving, grabbed a pillow and hugged it in front of her. Les kicked the coat over to the man half lying on the floor. Then he turned and looked at her. She was white-pale in the dim light, her face stained and puffy, her hair tangled and confused. Her eyes were wide with shock. Unfocused, they stared through him.

"Are you alright?" he asked stupidly.

She turned her face to the sound and looked at him. She opened her lips slightly to speak but just nodded dumbly and slumped her head into the pillow. He waited for her to say something, but she didn't. She just lay back into the bed and curled up on her side, clutching the pillow to her like a lover. He watched her for a few seconds and then, overwhelmed with angry, he turned to the man on the floor. He grabbed him up by the arm and pulled him through the door and across the landing. He pushed him down the first flight of stairs, heavily chasing after him and half dragging him the rest of the way. At the street, Les shoved him out the door and watched him stumble into the gutter. He went after him, grabbed him by the shoulders and threw him up against the wall. And then they were face to face, blood and fluid dripping out of the man's nose, his eye and cheek already grotesque yellow and swelling.

"Don't ever come back here," and his voice was low with menace.

Les let the man go and pushed him forward. For a few seconds, he stood reeling and then finding his feet he staggered away. Les stood in the light of the doorway. There was nothing in front of him but the cross-light night and his own shadow, confused and blurry. He swallowed, the adrenaline sick rising in his throat, and he leaned on the door frame, his legs shaking. He could see her curled on the bed and he knew he should, but he just couldn't. He gagged on the courage it would take. Then he simply reached back, closed the door behind him, and stepped into the night.

"Now I really have to leave," he thought, wiping his cheeks with his hand. He saw the small, dried stains of blood on the cuff of his shirt. He wondered...

"Monsieur La Clef!"

The voice was familiar. He didn't have to turn around.

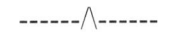

------/\------

A sneak preview of

No Safe Harbors:
An Emily and Dreyfus Adventure

Chapter One -- Wednesday

Emily knew he was back right after she opened the door. There was nothing to tell her that, no suitcase in the hall, no jacket flung over the chair, but she knew he was there. It might have been a scent or a subtle taste in the air, but mostly she just knew his presence. She was glad he was back. He had been gone less than a month, but it seemed longer. She had missed him. She always missed him. She dropped her keys and sunglasses on the table in the hall, kicked her sandals under it and stepped around the corner. The sun slanted brilliantly through the tall glass doors, turning the glossy wooden floor into shining honey. She could see him sitting silhouetted on the terrace over the river. She moved through the room, not quickly but certainly faster than when he wasn't home; trying one quick little girl foot slide across the floor before she asked.

"Hello?"

Dreyfus moved slightly as she went through the open doors. Caught in the sunlight, she stopped to refocus, then stepped forward and leaned down over him. She didn't kiss him but put her face next to his cheek and neck and took a long breath in through her nostrils, sniffing. She held her breath for a second and exhaled. He smiled and kissed her on the cheek.

"How was your trip?" she said, straightening up.

He didn't answer but indicated the drink tray on the low wrought iron table beside him.

"Yes, please," she said, smoothing the back of her full skirt with the palms of her hands as she sat down.

"Bloody awful. It's getting so I don't even like Asia anymore." He paused and handed her, her drink. "Not really, but you know what I mean."

"What time did you get in?"

"No idea. I'm still running on Shanghai time. I took the train. Baggage and passports and that – I imagine about 3:00. Actually I just got here. What is it now?"

"Just gone seven."

He looked at his watch and went to take it off but hesitated and dismissed it with his fingers.

"I'll get it later," he said and swirled his drink.

"Are you hungry? I can fix you something." She paused, "I think?"

He shook his glass.

"Do we have ice?"

She shrugged a tentative I don't know.

"Not to worry. Let's sit for a minute. Gerard's maybe? It's quick and easy. What do you think?

"I can ring them. See what he's got."

"No need, I'm sure we can get a table, and as long as it doesn't wiggle, I'm fine. You?"

"I had lunch with Tina and Mark. You know, awllll afternoon"

They sat together in the falling sun and spoke back and forth. The river moved below them and they watched the traffic. At some point, a tour boat chugged by, and they raised their glasses, mouthed a couple of obscenities and waved. A couple of water-winded tourists waved back.

"Did you get the gallery finished?'

"Barely. The opening's Thursday. Tina is, and forever will be, the world's biggest pain. You can't imagine..."

"Actually, I can," he said. "Oh! I brought you something."

He reached back and down for a black leather case by his chair and winced with the effort, the pain noticeable on his face. She leaned forward and lifted herself up, automatically reaching to help him. He stopped and put his hand out.

"It's alright," he said. "I fell down some stairs. Nothing serious"

She wrinkled an eyebrow but didn't say anything.

He turned out of his chair so he didn't have to twist and manipulated the case so the bottom slid open.

"Duty free," he said.

A flat velvet box dropped from the hidden compartment. He turned it in his hand and reached it across to her. She leaned forward so he didn't have to.

"I bought it for the green dress."

One-handed, she tucked her hair back from her face and lifted the lid. At first glance it looked like a large lump of flat jade, roughly polished, deep green and irregular; but when she picked it up, she saw that it hung from a chain made from the same single stone, completely linked, and cut -- one piece -- with the pendent.

"Open it."

She turned the precious thing in her hand.

"How?" she said

He smiled, "There's a latch on the bottom. Just squeeze a little bit."

She turned it over again and found a tiny silver sliver that looked like a vein in the rock. When she touched it, the stone jumped open in her hand, like a book, and inside a clock had been carved out of the interior. The green hands were bright against the deep white pearl face.

"My goodness!" she said. "You did miss me."

Later, they lay together in the half light that the city night cast through the loft. She held her head carefully on his stomach, neatly avoiding the huge purple and gold bruises that ran across his ribs. The breeze from the river was cool and they half dozed.

"I have to tell you," she said. "I bought a television set."

He stretched his shoulders, yawned, moved his head and pushed his hand through her hair to the back of her head, combing it through his fingers.

"And I seem to have acquired a lover."

His hand twitched imperceptibly and he continued combing at her hair.

"What are you going to do?" he asked

"Well, I'm not certain. He doesn't seem to want to take no for an answer."

He laughed and groaned, instinctively reaching for his ribs. She lifted her head and turned on her elbow to see him.

"I meant the television," he said.

"Oh! I thought the guest bedroom – for my mother -- unless you're dead-set against it."

He shrugged. She reached out and gingerly touched at edges of the bruises.

"Are you going to see about this?"

"I'll ring Barkely in the morning and let him take a look at it."

"Lots of stairs in Shanghai?"

"Not very many," he said.

Later, he eased himself off the bed and away from her. She moved and mewed into the pillow. He pulled on jeans and a sweatshirt and padded down the open stairs, out through the house to the terrace and the big night. Although the city never slept, the river was quiet and cool after the warm day, and the lights played out across its shivering current. He poured himself a drink and watched the tiny sparkling dancers.

"Why the hell did she buy a television set?" he thought.

Halfway around the world in a Seattle suburb, Milton Woodley and Stanley Parker waited nervously to leave. They had never been in the conference room before, and it seemed huge to them. Hidden in the basement of a midsized computer complex, they hardly knew it existed. It was interrogation-bright, with stiff, tall, uncomfortable chairs. The table was a big, matte black kidney, solid enough to make Milt wonder briefly how they got it in there. There were no decorations or adornments. This was a bunker for business. On one wall, there was a gigantic window that wasn't a window, because, on this day, they were looking deep into the Amazon rain forest. The opposite wall was covered in floor to ceiling wide wooden blinds and a single orange door, all solidly closed. But the room faced the third wall and a real time, larger than life video screen where the big boys played -- and they were clearly getting very angry. To Milt and Stilt, it looked like the three huge men on the screen were shouting directly at them, and they were worried about it.

"Explain to me again how this doesn't work. We own problem solving, for Christ sake. Analyze it, isolate it, integrate it, bury it -- I don't care. Just fix it."

"I already told you: we can't. It's gone."

"Gone! You keep saying that. Gone? Gone where? This shit doesn't just disappear. There's a line, a trace, something. Where's the computer?"

"In isolation." Jonah Talbot, the head of Security, measured his words. "We don't know if this thing, whatever this thing is, has wireless capability."

"Get somebody in there and go through it."

"You're not listening. We've done that. We've already gone through it, circuit by circuit.

All the software. All the hardware. Everything. But there's nothing there.

"Bullshit! Who was ground zero on this one? Now, everybody else just shut up and let me hear this."

Milton's voice sounded strange, as he heard himself speak, hollow and nervous.

"I got this e-mail at like noon. All it said was: Give me 120 million dollars or I'll destroy your corporate nation. Here's a demonstration. $E=MC^2$ No attachments, no nothing. Boom! That's it. I'm dug into the new Spectrum program, so I just flip it and go on. I figured I'd show it to Joe – uh -- Mr. Talbot, later. So about an hour later, I notice there's a blip in one of the variant colors. Nothing serious, but the waves don't match. I go back and check, and everything's fine but the blip's still there. So I run a history and there's a calculating error. Eight and four equals thirteen. So I got scared. I flip back to the e-mail, and it's gone. At this point, I freak and shut everything down -- like right now -- and phoned Joe. That's it."

There was dead quiet in the room....

WD Fyfe

Before WD called himself a writer, he worked at a number of different jobs -- from stacking lumber to interior design. He studied English at UBC and creative writing at ASU (where one of his teachers, Rita Dove, taught him the importance of the tale.) He has written for radio, magazines and newspapers, but never television. He's published both fiction and nonfiction in Great Britain and the US. He thinks he reads French passably, is working on his Dutch and speaks enough Spanish to get from A to B and find the toilet. He has interviewed John Cleese, Peter Ustinov, Margaret Drabble, Kenneth Branagh and enough other famous people to make him a hopeless name dropper. His not-so-secret passions are history and trivia, and he has never lost a game of Trivial Pursuit — although he did come 4th one drunken Quiz Night at the Uxbridge in Notting Hill, London. He lives on the Pacific Ocean -- but not close enough to see the water. So he spends his days writing a blog twice a week (www.wdfyfe.net) and working diligently on a novel, *No Safe Harbors* (a Dreyfus and Emily adventure.) It's a wonderful life, and he has only one regret: *he can't type faster*.

Made in the USA
Charleston, SC
04 December 2016